Lock Down Publications and Ca$h Presents

I0664147

HUB CITY
MENACE 4
Immortal Gangstas

Written By
J. WHITE

First Edition 2025

Printed in the United States of America

Lock Down Publications
P.O. Box 944
Stockbridge, GA 30281
www.lockdownpublications.com

Like our page on Facebook: Lock Down Publications
www.facebook.com/lockdownpublications.ldp

Stay Connected with Us!

Text **LOCKDOWN** to 22828 to stay up-to-date with new releases, sneak peaks, contests and more…

Like our page on Facebook:
Lock Down Publications

Join Lock Down Publications/The New Era Reading Group

Visit our website:
www.lockdownpublications.com

Follow us on Instagram:
Lock Down Publications

Email Us: We want to hear from you!

PART I

"What Goes Around"

Chapter 1

"Revelations"

The rhythmic thumping of the subwoofer vibrated through the floor of the mansion's massive media room, a low, pulsing bassline that accompanied the roar of the crowd on the massive screen. Patrick Mahomes, a Lubbock hero and Texas Tech football legend danced in the pocket, evading a blitzing defender, and launched a laser downfield. Jax, leaning forward in his plush recliner, let out a whoop, the smoky haze of his joint curling around his head.

"Hell yeah, that's what I'm talkin' 'bout!" he yelled, slapping the armrest. "Mahomes ain't playin' no games tonight!"

The sensational aroma of pizza, sliders, and hot wings mingled with the pungent scent of marijuana, creating a comfortable, almost nostalgic atmosphere.

Jax reached for his phone, the screen lighting up with an incoming call. "Hmm," he muttered, recognizing Terry's number. He tapped the green icon, bringing the phone to his ear. "Yo, T.J., what's good?"

"Jax, my nigga! How you doin', fam? How's everything been?" Terry's voice
was warm, almost overly so.

"I'm straight, man. Just chillin', watchin' the game," Jax replied, his eyes still
fixed on the screen.

"That's what's up, that's what's up. Just wanted to check in, make sure you

were good. You know, with everything that's been goin' on, I been thinkin' 'bout

you..." Terry paused.

"Yeah, man, I appreciate that," Jax said, taking another greedy pull of smoke. "Everything's been real rough, but shit, I'm still here," he blew out.

"I can imagine, bro. I can only imagine... Look, I know you're probably busy, but I was wonderin' if maybe we could link up sometime soon. Catch up, you know? In person."

Jax thought on it for a second and saw no issues, suspected nothing. "Yeah, man, that sounds good. Why don't you come through here to the crib?"

"For real? Tonight?" Terry's voice perked up.

"Yeah, man, come on through. We can talk about everything. It has been a minute. And I been meaning to get with you, just had a lot on my plate," Jax voiced.

"A'ight, a'ight, I feel that. Ain't no thang. I'll be there soon." Terry's voice held

a strange mix of patience and urgency. "Peace, bro."

The line went dead. Jax stared at the phone, a knot tightening in his stomach. He took another precious inhale. Not too long after, the doorbell chimed, a sharp, intrusive sound that cut through the room. *Damn, that nigga got here fast,* Jax thought, a flicker of surprise mixed with unease. He rose from his recliner, a sense of anticipation washing over him. He moved towards the door, his footsteps heavy.

He reached the door and took a deep breath, steeling himself for whatever lay on the other side. He turned the handle and pulled the door open. Standing on the doorsteps, bathed in the soft glow of the light, were two figures. Tuck, his face a mask of his usual street-hardened stoicism, and beside him, Dillon DeCair, one of the most formidable lawyers in Texas, his sharp suit and even sharper eyes cutting through the night.

"Aye, my nigga... man, I'm so glad to see you, fam," Jax exclaimed, a surge of relief washing over him. He reached out and wrapped Tuck in a powerful G-hug.

He released Tuck, then turned to Dillon DeCair, extending his hand. "Mr. DeCair, always a pleasure. Thank you for everything." He appreciated this man for the numerous times he'd saved him or one of his own from the confines of the tainted justice system.

Dillon DeCair shook Jax's hand firmly, his gaze steady. "Jax, it's good to see you. We managed to navigate the situation, as you can see." He gestured towards Tuck. "Technically, Tuck is free. All charges dropped. He's in no jeopardy of being bothered with this particular case again."

Jax let out a relieved sigh. "That's great news, man. I was worried like a muhfucka."

DeCair's expression turned serious. "However," he continued, his voice low, "Getting off on a crime of this magnitude...it doesn't go unnoticed. It puts a target on his back. Especially if he chooses to remain in the city. There will be eyes on him, Jax. And not all of them will be friendly."

Tuck nodded, his face grim. "I know, DeCair. I ain't stupid."

"Just be cautious, Tuck," DeCair advised. "And Jax, I'd suggest you do the same. This situation has ripples."

Jax nodded, his mind racing. He knew DeCair was right. Getting Tuck off the hook was a victory, but it was also a declaration of war in a sense. And declarations had consequences.

"Come on in, man," Jax said, gesturing towards the living room. "Let's talk about this inside."

Tuck stepped into the mansion, finally taking a deep breath of fresh *free world air* and exhaling, a wave of relief washing over him. He felt a sense of peace he thought would elude him forever. He was excited to be free, back on the outs, and around Jax, who had been through so much recently. He remembered when Jax gave him a leg up some years back, and just off the strength of that alone, he planned to have Jax's back through whatever storms lay ahead.

"Man, I can't believe I'm out that bitch, cuz," Tuck said, his voice filled with a mixture of disbelief and gratitude. "I thought a nigga was done for. But nigga, of all the things…that bombing…that shit was a miracle. Straight up divine intervention or some shit. On God." He shook his head, a look of awe on his face. "Fire destroyed the evidence room, and just like that… Without that evidence, they had nothin' on me."

Jax listened, his expression carefully neutral. He and Big D had orchestrated the bombing, but for entirely different reasons, tied to the complex web of their own struggles. He kept that knowledge to himself.

"I heard about everything that went down while I was locked up," Tuck continued, his eyes meeting Jax's. "Man, that shit crazy. I don't know what's all true and what ain't, but I want you to know…I'm ridin' with you, Jax. Whatever you need. Just say the word." He paused, a flicker of fierce loyalty in his eyes. "You been through a lot, bro. Lost a lot. But you ain't alone. I got your back, no matter what."

"My nigga!" Jax responded, a genuine smile spreading across his face. He reached out and they dapped up, a firm, brotherly handshake. "Appreciate that. It means a lot."

"No doubt."

"So, what's good, my nigga? You fresh out, now you're here. We got a lot of shit to do and catch up on businesswise, but we can get to it soon. But right now, what do you need?" Jax asked as if he were a genie who could grant any wish.

Tuck let out a weary sigh, his shoulders slumping slightly. "On the cool, man, I'm tired then a bitch," he admitted, a flicker of exhaustion in his eyes. "Really just wanna shower, throw some different clothes on, and get some rest. Start over tomorrow, get things right."

Jax nodded, understanding. "I feel that, Tuck. You've been through it too. This place is home, ain't nothin' changed. You know whatever you need is here, nigga. Do you," Jax stated with a wave of his hand. "You can kick it in the pool house if you need some more room," Jax added. "I got my lil brother with me right now, put him in a room on the second floor for his stay for a few days. He cool. It's plenty of other rooms and shit you know that, but I understand if you need you a lil space from other folks for a lil bit, know what I mean?"

Tuck skipped over the pool house part, his attention zeroing in on the "brother" part. He was confused. He knew all of Jax's immediate family, and the only brother he ever had was Marcus, whose terrible fate was known to the entire world. Greedy and D. Lee were like brothers too, but he knew their story, a blow that damn near crushed him when he heard about it. So, who was he referring to? "Brother?" he questioned, giving Jax a weary look.

Jax gave him a reassuring look and answered, explaining, "After my mother's passing, I learned about my biological father and decided to find and get to know him a little bit. Discovered I have a big family on my father's side, a few brothers close in age. Tyreke got with me this weekend to bond or what not, and it's just a surprise to see you in the flesh again too." Jax commented, "Lost a lot of family, but I'm gaining some too." His chest felt warm.

"Shit, that's wassup, man," Tuck replied. "What y'all boys got going on right now?"

"We just chillin', man, watching the game. You know, Pat Mahomes on that ass, and this nigga bucking the future GOAT," Jax capped.

Tuck replied comically, "Yeah, lil bro trippin'."

Jax said, "Shit, you wanna come up with us for a bit? Have a drink, we still got pizza and wings, all that. Know I keep that pressure too, shit, wassup?"

Tuck thought about it for a second but respectfully declined, saying he was just gonna do him for the night. He would get with them in the morning and start the day off right. He gave Jax his appreciation. "I can't wait to meet Tyreke," and cracked an inside joke with Jax as he departed, asking, "Do you and your brother look alike?"

Jax responded, "I ain't even gon' lie, we kinda do, fam. Our genes strong then a muthafucka," with a laugh.

Tuck laughed even harder, saying, "Aw shit, that nigga look like evil John Legend too."

That laugh shared was good for their souls but would be shortly enjoyed.

***

Jax returned to the media room to find Tyreke still holding on to faith Josh Allen would pull off a victory in the game. And to Jax's surprise, it looked almost as if he just might win. But he knew better. With only a few seconds left, Patrick Mahomes displayed yet again his unbelievable talents to the world and somehow managed to pull off the win with just a few incredible plays. He incorporated a few of the big-name stars in red, white and yellow alongside him, from the likes of Travis Kelce and company.

"See, that's that bullshit shit right there," Tyreke said, trying to cope with the
loss and hurt of a passionate fan whose soul just got crushed by their opponents.

Jax didn't rub it in too much and just stated to Tyreke that he may not see it yet, but Pat was the GOAT and to never buck him. Despite what anyone said, riding with that man, the odds were in your favor for the win every time.

Playfully, Tyreke said he was disgusted and that game made his stomach hurt. But in all actuality, it was from all the food he'd eaten during the game, and them spicy hot wings truly did him no justice. He slowly started to regret some of his choices that day as his stomach began to bubble like lava. He knew for damn sure what time it was.

"Yeah, whatever nigga," Tyreke said, rising from his seat. "I don't like how that game turned out, and I'ma go leave my review in your bathroom. Gimme 'bout thirty-five— forty-five minutes," he joked. "Bout to go up in here and see what that golden toilet hitting for."

Jax laughed more and told him, "Don't wear out your welcome in that muthafucka," as Tyreke disappeared down the hallway. "Spray is up under the cabinet!"

He shook his head, still chuckling at Tyreke's antics, and picked up the remote to lower the volume on the screen. The crowd still yelled and chanted in celebration of victory as color coordinated confetti rained down from above. He was reaching for his lighter to set fire to the joint he picked up off his weed tray, and before he could strike the BIC and ignite it, the doorbell chimed again.

***

Meanwhile, upstairs, Tyreke sat on the throne with his pants bunched around his ankles, iPhone in hand, scrolling through memes and snickering like a kid that was home alone. The bathroom was immaculate and spacious, with a gleaming gold toilet. But unfortunately, its grandeur was being diminished by the aftermath of Tyreke's stomach.

He groaned, leaning forward with a grimace. "Damn, them muthafuckin' hot wings... I ain't built for this, bruh..." he muttered to himself, waving a can of air freshener around like it was holy water. A loud *pssst-pssst* filled the room as he sprayed recklessly, making no real improvement of the scent. The toilet paper roll wobbled when he yanked at it, and he stared at the single-ply insult in his hand. "Man, this cheap-ass toilet paper. Might as well be wiping with receipts," he grumbled, shaking his head. Nigga got millions and still buying Dollar Tree tissue is crazy work," he vented.

He was just settling in for round two when a loud *BANG!* rang out from somewhere in the house. A single gunshot. The kind that freezes time. Tyreke froze mid-wipe, the air freshener still in his free hand, finger hovering above the trigger. His eyes went wide, heart thumping as silence settled over everything. No more jokes. No more dumb memes. Just that eerie stillness that comes after something real. "The hell was that?" he whispered to himself.

Slowly, almost reluctantly, he stood, still half-dressed, and crept toward the bathroom door. He cracked it open just enough to peer into the hallway, with his breath caught in his throat.

***

Shortly before the shot, Terry stood in front of Jax's home, eyes sweeping the expansive estate like a seasoned predator scoping the edge of the jungle. He was locked in, moving on nothing but faith in the power karma holds, pure anger and instincts, mimicking the portrayal of real killers he'd read about in urban novels, seen in old gangsta movies or some glorified character from the *Power* Universe.

Slowly stepping forward, he reached into the inside pocket of his designer crossbody bag and pulled out a small matte-black device—no bigger than a deck of cards. A quick press of the button, and a soft green light blinked to life. Cell signals, nearby surveillance feeds, neighborhood Ring cams—jammed. Or so he thought.

What Terry didn't know was that Jax had a fail-safe, high-end satellite video system that ran independently on an entirely different frequency, directly feeding footage to Big D's secure network in their hideout. It was a rare, almost paranoid setup—one Terry hadn't accounted for, and one that would prove to be a critical oversight, considering how far he was about to take things.

Unaware of the slip, he stashed the jammer back into his coat and stepped to the door. He adjusted the bag comfortably over his shoulder, the weight reminding him of the reason he came. As his finger pressed the doorbell, he steeled himself with a breath, already rehearsing the lines that were long overdue for delivery. This wasn't just a visit—it was a performance with a loaded punchline.

***

Even after everything Jax had seen—done, every betrayal, every bloodstained memory, every time he'd stared death in the face and cheated it—nothing could've prepared him for what was waiting on the other side of his front door... *Truth!*

His instincts were sharp, his senses were tuned, and a heavy piece stayed tucked in his waistband like a loyal dog. Still, as he approached the door, he wasn't expecting the devil to smile right in his damn face. The moment he turned the lock and cracked the door open, Terry's face abruptly greeted him with a calm, sinister grin—one that sent a warning too late.

Before Jax could even register it, a flying fist of fury came crashing into his nose with bone-rattling force and lightning speed. A sickening crunch followed with a vivid explosion of white light—like fireworks going off behind his eyes. His vision blurred instantly, blood gushing down his face as he stumbled back, barely upright. The pain was staggering. It didn't just hurt—it disoriented him, shook his equilibrium, and stole the clarity he relied on and needed in crucial moments like this.

Instinct kicked in before reason could. One hand clutched his face and the other went for the heat at his waist. He didn't see Terry, couldn't see much of anything, but his fingers wrapped around the grip, with his index on the trigger. With a desperate jerk, he pulled it back and fired in the direction of his attacker!

The sound ripped through the hallway of the mansion, a sharp, echoing thunderclap that raced through marble and hardwood, vibrating up walls and down the corridors.

***

"The fuck goin' on…?" Tyreke muttered under his breath, pausing for a half-second, sure he really just heard what he thought he did. There was a brief silence afterward. No screams. No shouts. No follow-up noise that he could really make out. Just the faint hum of the ventilation system and the slow drip of a leaky faucet.

He eased the bathroom door open with deliberate care, poking his head out like a soldier peeking from behind cover. His face was serious now. Not scared—Tyreke didn't *do* scared—but focused. Cautious. The kind of alert that came from growing up in neighborhoods where loud bangs usually meant someone had just lost a heartbeat.

He stepped out barefoot, walking as soft as a cat on the hardwood, back hugging the wall, ears straining. He didn't know where the shot came from exactly, or who it involved—but he damn sure knew something just popped off.

***

Jax could barely register what was happening—his world was spinning—ears were ringing. Pain radiated through his face, sharp and hot, as blood poured from his nose. His vision was smeared and doubled, like looking through a cracked windshield in the rain. He blinked hard, trying to will his sight back into focus, to make sense of the blur in front of him.

When the puff of gun smoke cleared, he realized the shot he fired had gone nowhere—hit nothing—and no one laid where he'd just aimed. Obviously, Terry was lucky enough to have gotten out the way. It was like he was fighting a ghost.

Before his mind could catch up, another flash of motion—*wham!*—a boot cracked across his face with the kind of violence that could end fights, end careers, end lives. The force of it spun his head and knocked him down like dead weight. A tooth—or maybe two—flew from his mouth. He tasted blood, coppery and thick, and for a split second, the world went dim.

Flat on his back, gasping and dazed, Jax felt the floor under him but couldn't feel his limbs. His body wasn't cooperating—everything inside him screamed to move, to get up, to fight back—but his body felt disconnected.

Terry stepped over him like a shadow with mass. Towering. Dominant. The look on his face was pure menace—cold, unbothered, like this was just another task on a to-do list.

Jax blinked again, the blur turning slowly into a figure standing over him and again, real fear began to creep into his gut.

***

Miles away from the chaos, Tory lounged in a dim-lit room, legs crossed, a half-empty glass of red wine swirling lazily in her hand. The oversized screen in front of her was lit up with a live 4K feed—every brutal second being broadcast through the tiny, high-end camera within Terry's designer Ray-Bans. She wasn't physically at the scene, but the crisp clarity of the image and audio made her feel like she was right there in the doorway, watching Jax's world crumble in real time.

She grinned, teeth flashing like a blade in the dark, eyes locked on the screen as Terry's black boot collided with Jax's face. The shot was so clean, so vicious, it made her flinch—then laugh. Tory was many things, but squeamish wasn't one of them. Watching Terry work was like watching a live-action masterpiece unfold—brutal, precise, beautiful in its own savage way.

Jax letting off that surprising gunshot scared her half to death, but when she realized her brother was okay and still engaging in this menacing attack, she relaxed. "I know that's right," she muttered to herself, smirking. "Get 'em. T." Through Terry's eyes, she had a front-row seat to the carnage—and from the safety of her location, she was loving every second of it. Revenge was sweet.

***

Terry stood tall over Jax, casting a long, warped shadow across the floor. Without hesitation, he drove his boot down into Jax's gut with a paralyzing stomp. The air exploded from Jax's lungs, sharp and involuntary, like he'd been stabbed in the chest with a steel spike. He coughed violently, eyes bulging, fingers clawing at the floor as his body buckled inward, desperately trying to refill his lungs. Terry's laughter echoed off the walls—low, ugly, soaked in malice—as he watched Jax writhe in pain.

"Ha-ha... now," Terry said, crouching slightly, a wicked grin cutting across his face. "I bet you wonderin' how you got here, huh, nigga?"

He tilted his head, eyes blazing with amusement and contempt, like a predator toying with a wounded animal. The moment was brutal, surreal—Jax still halfway between unconsciousness and full awareness, every nerve in his body screaming. Through the haze of pain, he knew this wasn't random. This was personal. Calculated. And far from over.

Jax was in no position to answer—and Terry knew that. But that didn't matter. He wasn't looking for a verbal response. What he wanted was to see the physical realization, the unraveling as the understanding spread across Jax's battered face like a slow, creeping poison. Jax's eyes were swelling, his breathing ragged, but Terry could see it, that burning desire to know *why*. And Terry couldn't wait to tell him.

With a grin still painted across his face, Terry took a single, deliberate step back. He reached into his crossbody bag, fingers moving with a knowing kind of reverence. When his hand came out, he held the answer—his truth, the missing piece of the fucked-up puzzle that had tangled their lives together.

He crouched low, knees spread wide, settling into a stance any seasoned gambling street nigga would recognize instantly. With a little flair, he shook his right hand back and forth a few times, the rhythmic clack echoing like a ghost of games past. Then, slick and smooth, he snapped his wrist and let them fly—two bloodstained, red-clear dice. They tumbled across the floor in front of Jax, wobbling as if time slowed to watch them land. The final result: *Seven.*

The sight hit Jax like a bullet through the soul.

As those dice came to a slow, haunting stop in front of his dazed eyes, something inside him fractured. Memories— vivid, raw, and cruel—slammed into his brain like a freight train. Blood. Screams. A night never forgotten. Faces long buried. The smell of death. And now, staring into the numbers, he understood. All of it.

Sick didn't begin to describe the feeling. It was like drowning in acid—slow, consuming, and inescapable. His body trembled, not just from the beating, but from the truth. The connection. The revelation.

And Terry? He just stood there, watching it all hit, smiling like he'd just hit the jackpot.

"Yeah, nigga," Terry said proudly, his grin stretching wider, sadistic pleasure dripping from every word. "Let that shit *sink in.*" He crouched down even closer now, his face just inches from Jax's, his breath hot with arrogance. The dice still sat there between them like a cursed relic, gleaming with blood and meaning. Terry tapped one of them with his finger, spinning it lazily as he continued.

"You remember now, don't you? Yeah... I *know* you do," he said, his voice

dropping into something darker, something colder. "Bet that shit hit you right in

the gut—just like I did."

Jax's bloodied face twitched, pain rippling through his jaw, his ribs, his soul.

The floodgates had opened, and the past came pouring through with no mercy. And Terry? He was loving every second of it.

"Thought that night was long gone, huh?" Terry sneered, standing tall again. "Thought you won. But nah, muthafucka... the house *always* wins. And in this case, nigga..." Terry growled, his voice trembling with rage and adrenaline, "I am the house."

Chapter 2

"What's Done in the Dark"

"See, *I* was in the house that night. 'Tha Spot.' Or whatever the fuck you wanna call it," Terry explained, voice sharp enough to draw blood. Each word dropped like a hammer as he carefully paced around his prey, his boots echoing through the foyer like a ticking clock counting down to something final.

His face contorted with fury, jaw locked, veins pulsing across his neck as his eyes bore into Jax. There was no hesitation now—no second-guessing. Just raw, volcanic emotion. The kind that had been boiling for years, buried under charm and fake smiles. Now it erupted!

"Yeah, I was there, muthafucka!" he roared, stopping mid-step, leaning down with a glare that could melt steel. "And I witnessed everything." His voice cracked with the intensity of the moment, spit flying as he barked that truth. The air around him thickened, charged, like the calm before a storm you can't outrun. Every syllable was soaked in resentment, and now that the dam had cracked, there was no plugging the flow.

"Everybody died that night," Terry went on, voice low but deadly. "And you just kept livin'—like their lives didn't mean shit. Like their screams weren't real, like that blood wasn't warm on the floor beneath your muthafuckin' shoes, nigga!"

He pointed down at Jax—bloody, broken, and dazed on the floor. Then he pointed toward the dice, still resting like cursed relics at the center of this confession.

"You rolled the dice, nigga. Knowin' you wasn't the only one who had a stake in the game… but you ain't give a fuck!"

Jax groaned beneath him, body twitching slightly, still struggling to breathe, to comprehend, to piece together this nightmare unfolding in real time. His lips were cracked and smeared in blood, nostrils flaring for breath, but he still couldn't muster words.

Terry crouched again beside him, voice dipping into a cold whisper. "I remember the screams...the smell of gunpowder…them niggas beggin' for they life while you stood there stone cold...like none of it mattered." He reached over and grabbed Jax's face, gripping it tight, forcing eye contact. "You made your move that night like the board was all yours."

Jax flinched in Terry's grip, trying to turn away—but there was nowhere to go. No escape.

Terry shoved his face down with disgust, then stood back up and resumed pacing. The floor beneath his steps was slick with tension—each footfall another beat in the symphony of vengeance.

"You thought the misdeeds of your past could just get buried beneath mansions, Rolexes, and power moves, huh? Thought all that street shit was behind you? Nah. All ghosts don't die in the transition, Jax. Some of 'em crawl back up out the dirt. And I'm *the one*."

He stopped in front of the dice, crouched down, and picked them up slowly, letting the blood on them stir memories. He held them out again, eyes locked on Jax's.

"These ain't just dice no more. They relics, nigga. You cursed 'em the night you spilled the blood of my brother on them and left 'em behind. You don't just get to walk away from no shit like that."

20

Jax finally found enough air in his lungs to wheeze, "Wha… what do you want?"

Terry's eyes lit up with something darker—satisfaction. He crouched down again, face way too calm.

"I want my muthafuckin' brother back," he whispered. "But since that ain't gonna happen? I'm gettin' everything else that's owed—pain, truth, balance. *Revenge,* nigga!"

He tapped Jax's chest twice—lightly, mockingly—like he was knocking on the gates of hell. His finger jabbing against the bruised flesh beneath the bloodstained shirt like it was the button to rewind time.

"You remember that night, don't you? Hell yeah, you do," he growled. "You might've tried to erase it—but I etched that shit in stone."

He stood up and started pacing again, his boots dragging slightly across the polished marble floor as if weighed down by ghosts. "I was just a shorty back then," he said, voice suddenly low, haunted. "Barely old enough to know what it meant to kill. But old enough to know what fear looked like on a grown man's face."

He stopped in front of a large window, his silhouette cast in the moonlight that spilled across the living room like a spotlight on a stage.

"They said that place is cursed," he continued, almost to himself. "That after what went down in that house, no energy could ever cleanse it. And they probably right. Because I carried that shit with me every fuckin' day after."

Jax groaned, shifting slightly. His mouth was thick with blood, but his eyes told stories his lips couldn't—of guilt, of realization, of a truth he thought would never have to acknowledge.

"You was there with that same look," Terry said, walking back over. "That same look like you ain't do shit. Like you ain't pull no trigger. But I saw you. I saw you!"

He kicked the wall behind him, making a picture frame crash to the floor and shatter like the moment itself had finally broken open.

***

The echo of shattered glass snapped Tyreke to attention. He had just cleared the second hallway, fist raised, heart banging against his ribs like a riot shield. Every creak in the floorboard felt like a landmine. He moved in tight bursts, low to the ground but ready, sweeping smoothly around dark corners. The mansion was a damn maze. Shadows danced in the corners. Thick, stale air hung over everything like secrets too old to speak. But that crash? That crash gave him direction.

Tyreke paused by a cracked doorway, head tilted as he zeroed in. The sound came from the east wing. He knew it had to be coming from there. He moved faster now, stepping over an overturned chair and ducking past a dusty chandelier that hung just low enough to catch a man slipping.

He kept his steps quiet, but his eyes were loud with urgency. Another muffled voice echoed down the corridor. Someone was yelling. Then silence again. "Fuck..." Tyreke muttered, doubling his pace. He was getting close.

***

Terry's voice was quieter now. Not calm—but surgical. Like every word was another incision on Jax's psyche.

"You stood over my brother's body like you were ready to make him a statistic. You ain't say no prayer. Damn sho' ain't offer no kinda help. You just shot him down, stepped over him like his name never meant nothin'. He leaned down again, this time pressing a hand against Jax's sternum and applying pressure.

Jax's chest heaved with shallow breaths, the pain almost too much to process. His vision flickered, shadows dancing in the corners of his eyes. But he kept listening—because he had to. Because whatever Terry was building toward, it was leading somewhere worse than the physical pain he was enduring.

"You ever seen your brother bleed out and you can't move? Can't scream? Just gotta sit in it? Just gotta listen to his breath get thinner and thinner, like the wind dyin' in the trees?" Terry's voice cracked, just a little. "I was behind the fuckin' couch, nigga. I watched that whole massacre, scared out of my mind and you left us all there like roaches in a puddle of Raid."

He shook his head slowly, stepping back and wiping a tear before it could fully fall. "But I never forgot you. I memorized your face, the way you walked, the color of your fuckin' hoodie." His laugh was bitter. "And when I seen you on the news a few years back—flashy suits, fake smiles, all that self-made mogul, 'Black Excellence' bullshit—I knew. I fuckin' knew then I had to make my move."

Terry walked over to a side table, calmly grabbed a bottle of water, unscrewed it and took a sip like he was just giving a TED talk. "You ever feel like the world gave the wrong people the microphone?"

He turned around, eyes burning. "They gave you the mic, Jax. Let you tell your version of the story. Turned yourself into a whole fuckin' brand out here. But you ain't never told nobody about 'Tha Spot' tho', did you? About things you really did in order to rise!" He tossed the water bottle next to Jax's head with a soft thud.

"I ain't here just to beat yo' ass," Terry said, now crouching again. "That

was just for fun. What I really want… is for you to hear this shocking truth. And dammit, hear me good."

***

The basement looked like a graveyard for the forgotten. Low ceilings, one flickering bulb, crates stacked in corners, and an old couch sagging under years of weight. Tina sat there, exhaling smoke, trying to calm her nerves with every drag. Angela scrolled through the static-y channels on the flat screen, half-hopeful, half-bored.

Big D leaned heavily over the table, whiskey in hand, staring as if the amber liquid might reveal answers. Life on the run had stripped everything down to bare bones—smoke, liquor, cards, and paranoia. The silence was thick enough to choke on. But the one thing that broke the monotony, night after night, was the live feed. Mounted on the far wall, an old monitor hummed with life, a live camera view of Jax's mansion, audio and video streaming to their hideout. It wasn't just a window—it was a secret line, mutual and untraceable, a lifeline connecting uncle and nephew. Big D could see Jax, hear him, even talk to him if needed, and Jax could do the same, a quiet tether across the chaos of their worlds.

The law-ducking trio watched it like it was scripture.

After a while with nothing happening on the screen, Angela squinted at the grainy image. "He's movin'… again."

Tina exhaled smoke sharply. "Where's he going now?"

Big D leaned forward, eyes narrowing. The feed was limited—one main camera covering the foyer—but the audio carried more. Every creak, every footstep, was magnified in their ears.

They watched Jax cross the frame, moving cautiously, eyes scanning, muscles tight as he approached the front doorway.

Seconds later, the silence was shattered. A sharp *pop* cracked through the speakers. Angela gasped, hand flying to her mouth. "Oh my God… that—" Big D's eyes locked on the screen. A tiny flash of light—gunfire reflected off the polished marble—then a dark figure blipped past Jax in a flash. The angle was imperfect, grainy, but it was good enough to catch a glimpse of what was happening.

Tina dropped her blunt, "Holy shit... that was a gunshot!"

Big D didn't need to see more. His pulse slammed in his chest. "I'm gone," he said, chair scraping the floor.

Tina jumped, panic sharp in her voice, "Wait...wait, D! You can't! You're wanted. Being hunted—"

His jaw tightened, eyes burning like embers. "And if I don't go?" He let that linger shortly. "My nephew's not dyin' on live feed on my watch. What you think I'm gon' do, just sit here and watch him get murdered?"

Angela's voice cracked, desperate. "D, what if you don't make it back?"

Big D's teeth ground together. "Then *I just don't.* But I'll be damned if my nephew dies while I sit watching."

No further words were exchanged. Hell, none needed to be. He said what he

said and he meant it.

Moments later, he was outside. The cold night air bit at his skin. The barn loomed like a shadowed monument. He ripped the tarps off the sleek Mercedes, dust and cobwebs rising in the moonlight. The Benz gleamed, ready! He slid in, engine growling awake, ready! One deep breath, then slammed the pedal. Tires screamed, gravel spat rocks, and the machine tore off into the night.

Thirty-four minutes from the city. He aimed for half that. Speed limits, cops, wanted posters—none of it mattered. Every second counted. He'd only seen the beginning of that footage and had no clue what Jax was enduring, but could only imagine. "Hold tight, nephew," Big D muttered, eyes burning as the speedometer climbed. "Unc comin'."

The countryside blurred into streaks of black and silver. The Benz roared over back roads, going at top speed. Every second meant Jax's life hung in the balance, every second could be the difference between surviving and slipping away.

***

The dream he was having didn't even make sense—just random flashes of noise, eerie shadows, and rapid gunfire. Tuck shifted on the couch in the pool house, shirt damp from sweat, mind twitching with memories that weren't even his. He blinked at the ceiling fan above him, slowly spinning like a clock that refused to tick.

Then the sounds came again. *Crash!*

He sat up, frozen for a second, rubbing his eyes and pressing the heels of his palms to his temples. "Too much stress, too much. That's all," he told himself to soothe his thoughts. But his gut said otherwise. It was similar to the knot he'd felt back in '06 as a small kid when bullets flew through his mama's window—it pulled at him now. Tight. Heavy.

Tuck rose, slow and cautious. The air in the pool house felt wrong now—too still, like it was waiting on something. He stepped to the door, barefoot, every muscle on edge. And as soon as he cracked it open and looked toward the mansion, he just knew. Something was *off.*

He didn't even think long. His boy was in there and he was going in. He didn't have a piece on him, not even a blade—but he moved. Quiet. Fast. Heart pounding. He crept up the side path, around the bushes, entering through the side door.

The second he stepped inside the mansion, he saw it. Jax—on the floor, bleeding. Bad. And T.J., standing tall. Gun in hand. Talking like a demon that finally made it to church.

Tuck ducked low behind a marble column, breath caught in his throat. His eyes darting, mind racing. He didn't think, he couldn't. This was bigger than him now. His boy was laid out like a sacrificial lamb, and the wolf was monologuing.

"I killed Greedy and D. Lee," Terry was saying, pacing like he was proud. "Cold blooded, huh? Yeah, that was me. *Me*, nigga. Let's see, oh yeah, had Kam's whip rigged up to

26

blow—made it look real good…that's me too, but not *all me*. I'll give credit where it's due… Does the name, *Bundle*, ring any bells? *Ha-ha…*" Terry laughed wickedly as Jax flinched with recognition of the name.

Tuck clenched his jaw. Every word another punch to the chest.

"I got Marcus set up on that fake-ass murder rap. Made sure the pigs smoked him in broad daylight. Another pawn off the board." Terry crouched back in front of Jax, real casual now. Like he was whisperin' bedtime stories. "And your mother? Hmm," He smiled something sinister. "You remember how all was well, then suddenly she started gettin' sick outta nowhere again when all this kicked off? Couldn't eat? Couldn't breathe right? That was me too. That poison hit her ass like justice, nigga!"

Jax twitched hard, lips cracked with rage but too weak to speak.

"Oh—and your baby momma?" Terry grinned, full of venom. "Oh, I did something really special with her because you really outdid yourself and pissed me off. See, you never knew this, but Lil Vicc had a son. Not a biological one but hell, with everything I ever been through, he was the closest thing I had to a father, and you decided to take that away from me. You and I both know what you did to him. And as fate would have it, I unfortunately had to bear witness to his demise as well right before my eyes… So, to be fair, I paid her off to disappear. Took Lil' Junior with her. You'll never see your son again. Lil bastard's gone. *Forever!*"

Tuck's breath hitched. His position was close now. Just a few feet from a clean line—he could rush him, maybe knock the gun away. Maybe.

"But my favorite all-time favorite accomplishment?" Terry chuckled darkly, standing up again. "Ke'. Your sweet, innocent, fine-ass baby sister? Yeah, she's pregnant… *With my seed.* We gon' start a brand-new family—once I kill you…"

That was it for Tuck. He moved like instinct. Broke cover and lunged. *"Aye!"* he screamed as he mustered all of his strength and focused it into a mighty blow. It connected slightly just as Terry spun around in time to deflect the force with the gun raised firmly.

BOOM! The shot echoed like thunder in a coffin under ground.

Tuck's motion wavered, he stumbled forward, breath catching as burning heat spread across his chest. He looked down, confused for a second, then saw the blood. Thick. Dark. Pouring. "Ah fuck..." he whispered, voice cracking. He fell to his knees, his eyes wide. Locked on Jax. A final look of apology. Of loyalty. "Sorry, my nigga... I tried to..." he croaked. And then he dropped.

Terry blinked—shook—but only for a second. Then the sick grin came back. "Guess I'll add that one to the list too," he muttered, nudging Tuck's lifeless body with the tip of his boot. "Rest In Piss, Tuck—another one down."

He stepped back over to Jax, voice tightening like a noose. "Now… it's your turn. The grand fuckin' finale."

Terry reached into the sleek black crossbody bag strapped across his chest—the same one that had been coughing up bad omens since he stepped foot in the mansion—and pulled out a squat, clear bottle filled with an amber-colored liquid. The label had been peeled off. No need for branding. The smell alone slapped the air. Sharp, chemical, flammable as hell. He uncapped it with a smirk, looking down at Jax like a preacher about to baptize a sinner in gasoline.

"See, you ain't just gon' die tonight, Jax. Naw... You gon' be erased. Like none of this ever existed."

He tipped the bottle, letting the liquid splash out in wide arcs as he walked. The scent of accelerant quickly took over the elegant space—fighting the rich cologne soaked into the marble and memories of cleaner days. He doused the floor in a deliberate pattern, wide and messy, every splash marking his intent in invisible ink that only fire would read.

Then, with no hesitation, he turned and dumped a heavy stream directly across Tuck's body. "Loyalty gets you killed," he muttered coldly. "Ain't that a bitch?"

The liquid soaked into Tuck's clothes, darkening them, pooling in the creases of his arms and chest. Terry didn't flinch. Didn't blink. Just kept it movin' like he was painting a masterpiece of vengeance.

Then he curved back around, circling Jax slowly like a wolf closing in on its kill. The last of the flammable liquid traced a full ring around him—tight, contained, symbolic. A trap with no exit.

Jax coughed, tried to lift his head, but his body failed him again. He was trapped in the eye of a storm, bleeding and bound by flames-to-be. The slick marble floor was slicker now. Slick with danger. Slick with the end.

Terry tossed the empty bottle aside. It clinked twice, then rolled into the shadows. He looked down at Jax with finality. "This... is your legacy. This is what you deserve. Bitch!"

Chapter 3

"Family Killin' Family"

The pain in Jax's chest was nothing compared to the weight pressing down on his pride. Terry stood across from him, that crooked grin stretched like it was carved into his face, gun steady in his hand.

"Nigga, you ain't half the man everybody think you is," Terry said, his tone low and sharp, like a knife sliding across glass. "Big bad Jax. Hub City's golden boy. But here you are, cornered, crawlin'… and about to die at my feet. Tell me, that sound like a king to you? No seriously, I feel like Michael B. Jordan in *Black Panther* when he was kickin' the shit out of T'Challa in that ceremonial battle… '*Is this your king?*'" Terry joked, his humor poorly taken.

Jax's breath came heavy, his arms trembling as he tried to push himself up from the floor. His eyes narrowed, fury burning brighter than fear. "You talk too much," he muttered, voice gravel rough.

Terry smirked, tilting his head. "Nah, I talk just enough. You need to hear this. You need to know you losin' everything before you check out."

The muzzle flashed twice—*BANG! BANG!*

Jax roared as fire shot through his legs. Both knees buckled instantly, his body collapsing in a heap. He clutched at his thighs, blood soaking through his jeans, warm and sticky between his fingers. The pain was blinding, but worse

30

than the pain was the realization—he wasn't moving. He wasn't walking out of here.

Terry stepped closer, savoring every second of it. His boots splashed in the pool of accelerant he'd already laid out across the floor, his steps deliberate, cruel. He crouched low, close enough for Jax to see the hunger in his eyes.

"This is how lions eat," Terry whispered, his voice almost intimate. "Slow. Watchin' life leave their prey little by little. You feel that, Jax? That helplessness? That's me takin' back everything you thought you had."

Jax spat blood on the floor, the defiance in his glare refusing to die. "Fuck you!"

Terry's laugh was short, joyless. "Oh, you gon' feel it, nigga. You gon' feel every second."

***

Upstairs, Tyreke had finally made it to the far side of the mansion. His chest heaved as he reached the top of the landing, sweat slicking his forehead. The closer he got, the stronger the stench in the air—something chemical, biting, an odor that made his nose sting. His stomach turned.

Then he heard it. More gunshots. Two. Loud, sharp cracks that rattled his bones.

He froze, his heart racing, then crept toward the banister that overlooked the wide room below. What he saw nearly ripped his soul out of his chest. Jax was on the floor, blood spilling across his jeans. And standing over him was a man Tyreke initially thought he'd never seen before—sharp features, eyes dark with hate. The gun was still smoking in his hand.

Tyreke's throat tightened. He wanted to move, to leap down, to do something, but his legs wouldn't obey. His eyes darted around the room, desperate for a weapon, anything— but he had nothing. He was unarmed. Too far away. And too late.

The man below—this intruder—pulled a lighter from his pocket, flicking the wheel with an almost casual rhythm. Click. Click. Click. A sick grin spread across his face as he held the flame above the accelerant-soaked floor. "No!" The word ripped out of Tyreke's throat before he even realized he'd said it. His voice echoed through the chamber, raw, panicked. "Don't do it!"

The intruder's head snapped up, startled. His grip faltered. The lighter slipped from his fingers and the world ignited.

Flames rushed across the floor in a jagged wave, heat exploding outward with a ferocity that stole the air from Tyreke's lungs. Jax screamed as the fire spread around him, encircling his body in a wall of heat. The intruder cursed, stumbling back as the fire caught his clothes. He smacked at himself frantically, fighting the small blaze licking at his side, before staggering toward the exit. And then—time slowed.

The intruder's face tilted upward, locking eyes with Tyreke. For a heartbeat, neither of them moved.

Tyreke's breath caught in his chest. The fire's glow lit the man's features, carving shadows across his cheekbones, his jawline. And in that instant, recognition punched Tyreke harder than any blow ever could. That face. He'd seen it before. Not in person, but in photographs buried deep in his father's boxes and one particular photo on the wall. Old, faded pictures of Mar and his brother Dre—two young men who looked like mirror images, both stubborn, both unbreakable. And sometimes, in the background of those pictures, were twins.

One, a boy, with the same sharp eyes, the same angular face. A boy who surely grew up to be this man.

Tyreke's mind spun. He didn't need anyone to tell him. He knew. Every bone in his body told him the truth. This wasn't just some random killer. This wasn't just an intruder.

This was blood. Uncle Dre's son was his cousin. Even if he didn't know it.

The realization hit him like ice water, his stomach twisting, his pulse crashing in his ears. He'd always known there was family out in Lubbock—his father Mar had mentioned it in passing—stories of Dre, of the life they'd lived and the roads they'd split on. Tyreke never thought much of it. It was just talk, history buried under years of silence and neglect.

But now? Now that history was standing in front of him, torch in hand, trying to burn his brother alive. Tyreke couldn't breathe. Couldn't understand. What could cause this? What twisted their bloodline into this moment?

He hadn't even known Jax long. Hadn't gotten the chance to sit down and learn all the family history, all the bad blood and broken ties. That was the whole reason he'd come to stay with Jax this weekend—to build that connection, to finally learn about his roots. But instead, he stood there, helpless, watching fire consume the room, watching his own cousin try to murder the one person who could have bridged everyone together.

To Terry, Tyreke was just another shadow in the room that would die along with Jax.

Tyreke's gut churned. His fists clenched at his sides. Blood or not, family or not, the truth seared into his brain, hotter than the flames climbing the walls. The man trying to kill his brother was his own cousin. And when Tyreke got the chance—he was going to kill that muthafucka—or die trying!

Chapter 4

"Beyond The Laws of Nature"

Big D tore through the iron fence like it was paper mache, the heavy frame of his car rocking against the broken bars, before he cut across the open lawn of Jax's massive estate. His breath was ragged, chest heavy, every instinct in him wired to one truth—something was bad, real bad.

The closer he got, the worse it became. Smoke curled out of the front wing of the mansion like a monster stretching to full size. Flames danced across the windows, orange and red shadows flickering against stone and glass. It wasn't just a fire—it was a blaze hungry to eat everything alive.

Big D exited the vehicle and rounded the corner, his Glock tight in his hand, out of habit. He was running fast and then—Bam! He collided chest to chest with Tyreke. Both of them staggered back, wild eyes locked. "—The fuck?" Big D barked, already raising the Glock.

"Wait! Wait! Wait!" Tyreke screamed, both hands flying up. His chest heaved, eyes frantic.

Big D's instincts screamed shoot first. His finger tightened on the trigger, but something about the kid's face stopped him cold. It was uncanny. The jawline, the set of his mouth, even the eyes. The resemblance was too much. He looked just like Jax and Mar.

That tiny pause, that breath between decision and regret, gave Tyreke the second he needed. "Man—my brother's in there! But the fire's too big—I can't get to him! You gotta help me or call somebody 'fore he burns! I dropped my phone when I..."

Big D said nothing. He just turned, sprinting for the flames. Tyreke hesitated, breath stuck in his lungs, before muttering under his breath, "Fuck it," and charging after him.

The front door was wide open. Not just cracked—it swung so far back it rattled against the wall. Through the opening, the blaze roared, flames licking the entryway, heat spilling outward like waves. Big D skidded to a stop at the threshold, his body jerking forward then stopping hard. He felt the heat against his skin, his mind calculating, debating.

Tyreke stumbled up behind him, sweat dripping, chest tight. "I tried, man! I swear I tried, but ain't nobody making it through that!"

And then it came.

A sound that pierced them both.

A scream.

It wasn't just pain—it was survival clawing its way out of a broken body. Jax's voice, raw and jagged, tore through the crackle of fire like a blade. It froze Tyreke in place. His stomach dropped.

But for Big D? That scream flipped a switch. With no warning, he bolted forward, headlong into the fire.

"Yo!" Tyreke shouted, stumbling back in shock.

But Big D wasn't listening. He pushed through the flames like they weren't even real, his massive frame swallowed in orange light. To Tyreke, it looked impossible—inhuman. The man moved like the fire didn't know what to do with him, as if it bent around him, sliding off his skin while his clothes caught the punishment.

Inside, Big D's eyes burned from the heat, lungs tightening as he scanned through smoke and flames. Then—there.

Jax.

Broken, bloodied, collapsed in a pocket of space the fire hadn't reached yet. His chest rose shallowly, his face twisted but alive.

Big D didn't hesitate. He scooped Jax up, body and all, slinging him across his arms like a child. Jax groaned faintly, head falling against Big D's shoulder. And then D turned back to the fire.

He hit it head-on. Flames licked at him, clawing at his arms, his back, his clothes. But again—like something beyond nature was watching—his skin wasn't touched. It was as if the fire knew who he was and stepped back just enough to let him pass.

Tyreke's eyes nearly fell out of his skull when Big D emerged. The man was carrying Jax, his massive arms wrapped tight, his shirt singed and his jeans scorched but his skin untouched. Jax's face was pale, eyes clenched shut, but his chest still rose and fell.

For one insane second, Tyreke thought he was seeing something out of the Bible—Moses walking through the Red Sea, but instead of water, it was fire. He stuttered, voice trembling, "W-what the…what the fuck did I just see?"

Big D didn't answer. He laid Jax down against the wall outside, then doubled over, gasping, eyes wild. He knew what had just happened. He knew it wasn't normal. But this wasn't the time nor place to touch on that subject.

Tyreke crept closer, staring, mind spinning. The fire. The madness. His cousin Terry's involvement. His brother Jax. The whole night was one big nightmare, and now he was standing next to a man who just walked through flames like a god or even worse, a demon.

Their eyes met. Neither spoke. It didn't need words, look said everything. This was real. But reality was still ugly. Jax was in bad shape. The mansion was still burning. And Big D? He was a wanted man with cops on his ass and enemies everywhere.

"Gotta move. Now," Big D growled, his voice low but urgent.

Tyreke's head spun. His hands patted his pockets on reflex. He pulled out keys—the Bugatti's keys, the ones Jax had tossed him earlier. But he froze. Two seats. No way three men fit.

He glanced around, mind racing.

Money. Power. Privacy. This was Jax's estate—there had to be more cars, probably untouched. He sprinted down the drive, past sleek coupes and glossy imports, eyes scanning. Too small. Too fast. Not what they needed.

Then he saw it.

Parked at the far edge of the lot, bulky and squared off under the glow of firelight—a Tesla Cybertruck.

"Please, please, please," Tyreke muttered as he yanked the handle. It opened. *Unlocked. Key fob inside.* "Thank God!"

He pressed a few buttons, held the brake and the engine came alive, tires kicking gravel as he spun back toward the burning house. He pulled up, heart in his throat and jumped out.

"Load him up!" he shouted.

Big D didn't waste a second. He hauled Jax up, muscles bulging, and slid him carefully into the back. Tyreke scrambled to help, shoving bags and junk aside to clear space. Jax groaned, eyelids fluttering, but still out cold.

Big D slammed the back door shut, chest heaving, face hard. He climbed into the passenger seat, eyes already scanning the road ahead. He looked at Tyreke, voice sharp, unshakable. "Now drive this muthafucka. Fast!"

***

Now far away from the burning mansion, Terry sat in his car, processing the night's events. The stench of smoke and accelerant still clung heavy to his clothing and the air around him, but he was so mentally high and thrilled from what he just pulled off, he was numb to the smell. The mansion's blaze reflecting in his dark sunglasses. In the back of his mind, he replayed those last moments before he made his exit and thought about the figure he'd seen on the steps, yelling at him. A witness he hadn't made sure was dead.

But the fire had done its work, he assumed. It was rising hot and fast, blocking escape and aiding his plan. Everything he intended to do had been executed. Now, all that remained was the final act with Ke'.

He didn't plan to hurt her—physically anyway. That wasn't the goal. He wanted the satisfaction of watching, waiting, timing everything perfectly. The sirens and choppers soon approaching the mansion would signal the show. He would be present in the room as Ke' learned about her brother and her heart would surely break. He would be her support, a comforting presence. She would love him. His psychotic ego swelling as he manipulated her emotions and kept control over the story.

Minutes passed. Each one stretched like eternity. He imagined stepping into the hotel room, Ke' looking up at him—innocent, unsuspecting—and him standing there, calm, composed, her panic unfolding at the exact moment he wanted to disclose things.

Every tear, every gasp, would be his to witness. That's how he wanted it.

Then, in the distance, he heard it. Sirens first, faint, then growing louder. Police. Fire. And above, the chop of helicopter blades.

His grin widened, slow and deliberate. Showtime. The culmination of his planning had arrived. Every lie, every manipulation, every calculated step had led him here. And now the moment of truth was coming.

He leaned back, savoring the pause, letting the tension swell. Then, finally, the signal he'd been waiting for—the chaos outside, the approaching response units. His cue.

Terry pushed the door open, planted his feet on the asphalt, and looked up at the hotel. The room number glimmered above. His chest rose and fell with anticipation. The chaos was about to unfold, and he would be there. Watching. Controlling. Orchestrating.

He stepped toward the hotel, ready to insert himself into the moment he had created, the final act of his carefully twisted script playing out to play out.

***

From the moment Big D left, Tina and Angela were glued to the screen. The electric hum of the surveillance equipment. Tina couldn't bring herself to breathe. The rational part of her mind, the part she had carefully cultivated for years, screamed that what Big D was attempting was an act of suicide, but given the current situation she understood there was no stopping him now.

They stood for what felt like an eternity, the only movement the slow, agonizing crawl of the seconds on the digital clock. Then, the first crackle of static came from the speakers. It was distant at first, a faint, popping noise. Then a louder sound, like two sharp claps of thunder.

BANG! BANG!

Angela's hand flew to her mouth, stifling a cry. "Oh God," she sobbed, her body starting to tremble. "Oh God, they shot him."

Tina's stomach dropped. She didn't need to see it to know. Those were gunshots. Muffled, but unmistakable.

The crackle on the screen grew louder, a roaring sound, then an angry, consuming roar. The image on the screen, which had been a clear-enough shot of the foyer, began to shimmer and distort. Waves of heat were hitting the camera. Then, a rush of orange and red light filled the frame, a jagged, living thing that ate up the hallway and spilled into the main room. The feed became a swirling, chaotic painting of fire.

"No!" Angela shrieked, pressing her hands against the screen as if she could push the flames back. "Please, no! Lord, have mercy!" Her voice was a wail, a raw, primal expression of a mother's fear.

Tina felt a cold, deep-seated dread. All the fear she had been holding back, all the hope she had been trying to build was now a sinking weight in her chest. She saw a flicker of a shadow move within the fire, a figure staggering, swatting at himself before disappearing. It was the last thing she saw of the man who had done this to Jax.

Then, there was nothing but fire. A wall of it. A living thing that seemed to breathe and writhe on the screen. It was so bright it cast a warm, orange glow across their faces, a hellish light in the cold quiet of the basement.

"He's... he's..." Angela whispered, her voice a hollow shell. She fell back, her legs giving out, and slumped to the floor, her hands shaking, her eyes overflowing with tears. She didn't look at Tina. She just stared at the screen, at the angry, all-consuming blaze.

And then... the camera flickered. A new shape appeared on the screen, a massive, broad silhouette moving in the distance, cutting a path toward the front door.

"Who is that?" Angela choked out, her voice filled with a desperate, tiny kernel of hope. "Is it... is it someone? Is it the fire department?"

Tina squinted, her eyes straining against the glare. The figure was too large for a firefighter, too quick. Her breath hitched in her throat. She knew that form. It was Big D.

He moved with a speed that defied his size. He was at the entryway now and the feed was a chaotic mess of smoke and flame. He paused for a fraction of a second, his body a dark, immovable shape against the inferno. And then, he did the impossible.

He walked into the fire.

It wasn't a brave dash. It was a purposeful step. It was as if he was walking

through a beaded curtain instead of a raging fire. The flames that had been licking

at the frame, roaring and pulsing, seemed to part around him. They bent. They slid.

They danced off his skin. For one impossible, surreal moment, it looked as though

the fire was afraid of him.

Angela gasped. Her eyes, which had been glazed with tears, widened in a mixture of awe and disbelief. She saw the same thing Tina did. The massive form, swallowed by orange light, but still moving forward, still whole. She started to mumble, a jumble of prayers and praises. "Oh, my God… He… He's walking through it! He's walking through the fire! Lord, you have sent an angel! A guardian angel! Please, let it be! Please!" Her voice rose with each word, a desperate, frantic chant.

But Tina felt no such relief. The sight of Big D was a punch to the gut, a cold, sickening wave of recognition that went far deeper than the hope Angela felt.

The moment Big D stepped into the fire, something within her, something she had suppressed and run from for a lifetime, stirred and roared to life. This was not God. Not an angel.

This was her mother's work.

An image flashed in her mind, the bayou back home, the thick, murky water, the Spanish moss hanging from ancient trees like shrouds. She saw her mother's hands, gnarled and powerful, mixing herbs and dirt. She heard the low, guttural chants that made the air feel thick and heavy. Her mother had spoken of "protection," of "shields" that could be woven from old magic, from ancestral debts. She had seen her mother do things that defied the laws of nature, things she had always dismissed as folklore, as old wives' tales told to scare city folks.

But now, she was seeing it for herself. Big D walking through fire… again. This wasn't his first time and couldn't be a coincidence. She denied the idea the first time out of convenience, since her life was saved during the act, even though her infidelity at the time was discovered in exchange. This wasn't a miracle. It was a testament. A terrible, horrifying proof that the world she had built, the respectable, clean-cut life she had tried so hard to live for the most part, was just a thin layer of paint over a much older, darker reality.

Tina's mind was a frantic whirlwind of thoughts. The memories of her mother's stories and practices, of the family legacy she had so vehemently denied, came rushing back to her in a terrifying torrent. She remembered being a young girl, watching her mother heal wounds that should have festered, seeing her commune with forces that made the hair on Tina's arms stand up. It was all real.

On the screen, Big D reappeared in the smoke-filled entryway, a dark mass of a man carrying another body. It was Jax. He was a limp weight in Big D's arms, but he was there.

Angela's sobs turned into frantic, grateful prayers. "He did it! Oh, Lord, he did it! Thank you! Thank you, God, you saved him!" She was on her knees now, hands clasped, tears streaming down her face in an act of pure, unadulterated worship.

Tina just stood there, her body rigid, her mind reeling. She felt a profound sense of relief, yes, but it was mixed with a terror that was new and far more dangerous than the fear of a fire. The world she thought she knew had just been burned away, replaced by a reality that was far more complex and terrifying.

Angela looked up, her face a mask of hope and wet mascara. "Did you see that, Tina? It was a miracle! It was a miracle!"

Tina looked at her, her eyes hollow. She could not lie. Not to herself, and not to Angela, not anymore. "No, Angela," she said, her voice a low, gravelly whisper. "That wasn't a miracle. That was something *else.*"

The words hung in the air between them, an ugly, profound truth that settled over the relief like a shroud. Angela's face fell, her smile dissolving into a look of profound confusion and fear. She had known bits and pieces about Tina's family history, beliefs and spiritual practices, but she had never taken it seriously. It was just a weird part of Tina's past. But now, seeing the chilling certainty in Tina's eyes, she knew there was something more here.

Tina walked to the screen, her finger tracing the now-still image of the burning mansion. She had to talk to her mother. She had to understand what this meant. This wasn't just a rescue. It was a reclaiming. Her mother had reached from a different world and placed a marker on their lives.

She looked at the screen, at the roaring flames, and a cold, terrible understanding settled over her. The fire hadn't destroyed anything that mattered. It had just cleansed the path for what was to come. The old, predictable world was gone. The new, supernatural one had arrived. She was no longer running from her past. Her past had just come to claim her.

And in that moment, she knew with certainty that this was just the beginning of another whole series of events that were sure to come.

***

Detective Crockette had long stopped believing in coincidence. Most nights, when the city finally fell quiet, when the dispatch chatter slowed to a crawl, something in his gut would push him toward the old backroads. He told himself it was habit—routine patrol, checking blind spots—but truth was, it was loyalty and a debt.

Jax had once done what no badge, no precinct, no courtroom could have pulled off—he'd saved Crockette's life and given him a clean slate with no worries. No more looking over his shoulder, he was cool. All thanks to Jax giving the cartel what they demanded when they were ready to carve him up like a hog. Crockette never forgot it. Couldn't. That kind of thing doesn't just wash off a man. It burrows in. Eats at you.

That's why this night, with his headlights slicing through the dirt road leading out to Jax's mansion, Crockette wasn't surprised when the air felt wrong. Heat shimmered against the windshield, even with the windows up. Then he saw it.

The sky above the property was painted in shades of hell—orange flames clawing out of shattered windows, smoke rolling like storm clouds, embers drifting across the field like fireflies from another world. The closer he crept, the louder the sirens swelled behind him. Units were inbound. Fire. Squad cars. A circus.

Crockette's hand drifted to his radio, but before he could even key it, a pair of headlights exploded down the entrance road toward him. A Cybertruck, big, mean, moving recklessly, chewing up gravel in a frenzy.

"Shit," Crockette hissed, snapping his wheel sideways. He cut his brights, let and let instinct take over. One hand drew down on his service weapon, and the other flicked his red-and-blues alive. He angled his cruiser across the road and braced.

The Cybertruck skidded hard, tires screaming against dirt, before lurching to a halt not ten yards from his bumper. Crockette stepped out slowly, gun steady, chest heaving with a cop's trained caution—but what came next damn near cracked him in half.

The driver's door swung open. Tyreke stepped out first, wide-eyed, young, too green to be in this much shit. But then the passenger door opened. And out climbed Big D.

He started to bark the standard order—*"Hands where I can see 'em!"*—but the words tangled in his throat when his gaze slipped to the backseat. A figure slumped, motionless, head lolling, face pale beneath the fire's glow. Blood smeared across his shirt. Jax!

"Damnnn..." Crockette muttered, lowering his gun completely.

Big D's eyes locked on his. They didn't speak. They didn't need to. A whole history of shared violence and silence stretched between them like a bridge.

Crockette swallowed hard, nodding toward the burning mansion. "What the hell happened?"

Big D's reply was clipped, sharp, the way men talk when time is bleeding out. "Family business. Jax caught the worst of it. We gotta move."

Crockette's jaw flexed. Sirens wailed louder, closer, painting the night in red and blue. He glanced over his shoulder, then back to them. Choices flipped like cards in his head—protocol, procedure, duty—but none of it mattered. Not compared to the man bleeding out in that truck.

He holstered his weapon. "No time. You ain't got thirty seconds before half the damn city's here. What's the address?"

Big D hesitated, testing him with his stare, then gave it up low. A safehouse. One Crockette didn't need to know but knew now.

"Alright," Crockette said, climbing back into his cruiser. His voice went tight, commanding. "I'll run the lead. You stick tight on my bumper. Don't stop for shit. Trust me."

Without another word, the engines roared. Red-and-blues lit up the night as Crockette whipped his cruiser forward, carving a path off the main road in the opposite direction of the incoming cavalry. The Cybertruck followed, Jax's blood painting the leather inside, the three men carried by momentum and desperation.

Seconds behind them, the first firetrucks pulled onto the scene. But the mansion's flames had already told their story—one of blood, betrayal, and a night the city would never forget.

Chapter 5

"Denied Deception"

The quaint hotel room was too quiet. Ke' burrowed deeper under the covers, a low groan rumbling in her chest. The first few weeks of pregnancy had been a constant battle between her stomach and her willpower. She was either nauseous or ravenously hungry, but mostly, she was just tired. Bone-weary in a way that sleep couldn't fix. The silence of the room, meant to be comforting, was now just a thick, lonely pressure.

She grabbed her phone, and the bright screen jolted her eyes. The contact list was short, but her thumb hovered over the top name. T.J. She had reserved the room for them both. *He was supposed to have been here hours ago.* A wave of irritation washed over her, and she felt the familiar pull to send a text, a gentle prod to ask where he was. *Just come on, babe. I'm exhausted.*

But then, she hesitated. He was working. He was building something for himself, and for their future. He had told her that.

So, what was the point of bothering him when he'd be here soon anyway? The thought of him showing up while she was staring at her phone, desperate for a message, seemed pathetic. No. She'd be fine. She exited the message thread, the little thought bubble of a text unsent, and then tossed the phone onto the nightstand.

She glanced at the television. The local news was on, playing silently, muted tones. She fumbled with the remote, turning the volume up. The face of a beautiful reporter, Gabrielle Renee, graced the screen, her expression a careful mix of professionalism and a barely concealed hint of personal emotion. The banner across the bottom read, "BREAKING NEWS."

"We are just receiving reports of a massive fire at an estate on the outskirts of town," Gabrielle began, her voice low and serious. "Sources on the ground confirm the mansion belongs to a prominent local figure, and we are hearing unconfirmed reports of..."

And then, a sharp, yet insistent knock at the door.

Ke's heart skipped a beat. She knew that knock. It was a familiar pattern, a rapid-fire series of thumps that only he used. A smile, slow and genuine, spread across her face, chasing away the fatigue. It wasn't the delivery guy. It wasn't room service. It was him. T.J. Her mood elevated at the thought of finally getting her hands on him, of wrapping her arms around his neck and forgetting about everything else.

She scrambled off the bed, smoothing her hair and pulling her robe a little tighter. She yanked the door open with joyful urgency. There he was, standing in the hallway, looking handsome and tired. "Hi," she said, her voice soft and full of relief.

"Hey, babe," TJ said, stepping into the room. He leaned in for a quick, sweet kiss, his hands settling on her hips. "I am so, so sorry. This session ran way longer than I planned. I didn't even get a chance to get with Jax either. Tried to call him, but I guess he was still tied up."

Ke' gave a light shrug, her smile undiminished. "It's fine, I'm just glad you're here now." She walked back to the bed, collapsing onto the pillows with a sigh of contentment.

"What have you been up to?" Terry questioned.

"Mostly working," she said with a tired grin. "And sleeping. But I just turned on the TV. Looks like some more

HUB CITY MENACE 4 | J. WHITE

stuff went down—they're just about to report on it." She gestured to the screen where Gabrielle Renee was still speaking, her voice a calm anchor in a brewing storm of information. "Seems like a lot of drama for one night, huh?"

Terry's eyes, hidden from her, flickered to the television. The timing was nothing short of perfection. The universe, it seemed, was his greatest co-conspirator. It couldn't have lined up better. He was present in the room, calm and composed, and she was seconds away from receiving the news he had orchestrated. He would be her rock, her shoulder to cry on, her protector in a moment of pure, unadulterated pain. Every tear, every gasp, would be his to witness. He had denied her the chance to find out on her own, instead controlling the entire narrative from within her emotional space. The script was playing out exactly as he had written it. He had a front-row seat to the culmination of his plan.

The deception was complete.

"Yeah, sure does," Terry said, his voice laced with a cold eagerness that Ke' was too exhausted to notice. He walked over and picked up the remote, holding it out to her. "But, shit, turn it up a lil more. Let's see what the city's on now."

Ke' took the remote and increased the volume, the news report now filling the quiet room. She was oblivious to the trap she was walking into, a web of deceit carefully laid by the man standing just a few feet away. On the screen, Gabrielle Renee's face, usually composed, now carried a weight that made her seem years older.

"This is Gabrielle Renee, reporting live from KLBK News Channel 13," the reporter said, her voice dropping to a somber, professional tone. "The scene behind me is one of complete devastation. Firefighters have been fighting the blaze for at least half an hour now, and authorities are still trying to make their way through the residence to see if there were, in fact, any confirmed casualties."

Ke' watched, her brow furrowing. She knew the estate. She'd been there countless times, but never like this. Never as a smoldering ruin. Her hands started to tremble almost imperceptibly as the camera cut to a shot of thick, black smoke still billowing from the remains of the mansion.

Renee's voice returned, carrying a more direct and painful punch.

"Authorities have confirmed the owner is, in fact, *missing,* and that he may have been caught up in this tragedy. The fire appears to have been deliberately set, with clear signs of arson, and a spent shell casing was found at the home's entrance."

Ke's breathing hitched. *Missing. A spent shell casing?* Her mind, groggy with morning sickness at night, began to clear. This wasn't just a fire. It was something else. Something malicious. The name of the owner was not mentioned, but she didn't need to hear it. This was Jax's house. She knew it in her bones. She turned her head slightly to look at Terry, who was watching the screen with a focused intensity. She wasn't suspicious. Just anxious.

Just as the camera cut back to Renee, there was a brief pause, a moment where the reporter's eyes flickered off camera as a voice spoke into her earpiece. Renee's composure, a carefully constructed façade of professionalism, began to crack. She took a deep breath, her eyes softening with a touch of authentic sadness before she delivered the most daunting information of all.

"And, I am now sorry to report," Renee said, her voice barely a whisper, a stark contrast to the urgency of her earlier report, "that while the identity cannot be confirmed at this time, authorities have recovered what seems to be the *extremely charred remains of at least one person.* However, the condition of these remains aren't in the best shape, based on initial reports."

For an unreal moment, the professionalism that had been Renee's trademark on live TV completely shattered. Her eyes glistened, her lip trembled, and she looked utterly devastated. The camera, in a frantic attempt to save the broadcast, quickly panned away from her to a field reporter.

When the screen cut away, Ke's life changed forever. She felt the blood drain from her face, her hands going numb as the remote slipped from her grasp and clattered to the floor. The nausea she had felt all morning returned, this time as a visceral, gut-wrenching pain. The words *extremely charred remains of at least one person* echoed in her head.

She couldn't believe what she had just heard. It was impossible. It couldn't be him. It couldn't. The room, which had seemed so safe just moments before, now felt like a cage. Her entire world was crashing down, and all she could feel was the overwhelming, all-consuming pain.

And with that pain, the world went dark. Her knees buckled and the floor rushed up to meet her, a black tide of unconsciousness washing over her.

***

She came to slowly, the world fuzzy around the edges. Her head was a pounding drum. She was in Terry's arms with her head nestled against his shoulder. His other arm was wrapped around her back, his hand stroking her hair.

He was talking softly, his voice a low, comforting rumble.

"It's okay, baby. It's okay. I'm right here. I'm here for you." He sounded choked up, his voice catching as if with tears. She could hear him sniffle. "I can't believe this… I just can't… I'm so sorry."

He squeezed her, pulling her tighter against his chest. For a fleeting moment, she found comfort in his embrace, a lifeboat in the turbulent sea of grief. She took a shaky, deep breath to steady herself. But as the air filled her lungs, a new sensation hit her, a jarring, unforgettable smell. It was the unmistakable hint of smoke and the acrid stench of chemicals, like gasoline or lighter fluids. It wasn't the room.

They were non-smoking per her preference. It was clinging to his clothes, a scent that shouldn't have been there. It was on his shirt, his jacket, even in his hair. The smell was all over him, like a grim, personal perfume.

And in that instant, a cold, sickening clarity swept through her. Her mind, foggy and weak from the shock, suddenly snapped into focus. She remembered the fire. She remembered the *gunshot casings*. She remembered the words, *"extremely charred remains."* And she remembered his calm voice, telling her to *turn the TV up.* It wasn't a coincidence. She could feel what was possibly a gun in his waist.

She'd just realized the nigga still had on sunglasses in the middle of the night. A lot of shit just wasn't right. It wasn't just some horrible twist of fate and coincidence. *It was him.* It was him all along!

The reality of the situation hit her with the force of a physical blow. Terry's comforting tears felt like acid on her skin. His touch, which had just moments ago seemed like a safe harbor, now felt like a predator's grip. She was in a locked room with the man who had murdered her brother. The realization was so profound, so utterly terrifying, that she could barely breathe.

She stiffened in his arms, her heart a frantic hummingbird against her ribs. She had to act fast. She had to get the fuck out of there. But where was she going to go? She had nowhere to run. But she surely wasn't about to be next.

Her mind raced. *Think. Think fast.* All the strength in her body had to go into a single, decisive move. She shifted, her body beginning to shake as if she were about to be sick. "I… I think I'm going to throw..." she mumbled, pushing against his chest. Her voice was raspy, barely audible.

Terry immediately recoiled, his face twisting with revulsion and concern. "Whoa, whoa, whoa. Okay, go! Go!"

Ke' scrambled off the bed, stumbling toward the bathroom. She didn't look back, not for a second. The door slammed behind her and the lock clicked into place, a flimsy barrier but one that, for the moment, felt like a fortress. She leaned her back against the door, her heart hammering.

Then she turned the faucet on full blast, water rushing into the sink to muffle any sound she made.

She paced the small room, her hands flying to her head. "Fucked," she whispered. "I am so fucked." She had nothing. Her keys, her phone and her purse, all her belongings were in the main room, with him. She didn't even have shoes on.

She was trapped. She looked up, her eyes scanning the room for an out. There it was. A small window, a square of dark glass in the corner of the wall. She lunged for it, unlatching it and pushing it open. It was small, but she could squeeze through. She peered out into the darkness. She was only on the second floor. A fall was better than staying in that room.

She took a breath and began to climb. She swung one leg over the sill, then the other, her body twisting to get a grip on the ledge. She was almost out when she heard a gentle knock on the door.

"Ke'? You okay in there?" Terry's voice was soft, laced with a feigned worry.

She had to buy time. She pulled her head back in just enough to make her voice sound closer. "Yeah, I'm okay. Just... a little dizzy. I'll be out in a minute," she said, her voice shaking with adrenaline.

She heard a sigh of relief. "Okay, babe. Take your time."

Ke' didn't wait. The second she heard his footsteps move away she scrambled to get back out the window. She was almost there, her feet dangling over the edge, when a deep, cold voice boomed from the other side of the door. "Ke'!"

Terry's gentle, fake voice was gone. This was his real voice. A crash followed, and the door splintered as he threw himself against it, the wooden frame breaking off the hinges. Ke' screamed, her body convulsing in a panic. She lurched, her feet slipping from the ledge, and she fell, a short but shocking drop to the ground.

She hit her back on the hard asphalt, the impact stealing her breath. She lay there for a second, a sharp, white-hot pain shooting through her spine. And then, as she fought to get up, she saw him. He was framed in the broken window above her, the hotel room's light casting him in a demonic glow. Their eyes met for a terrifying moment—his were wide with a mix of fury and confusion—hers were filled with pure, unadulterated terror. He knew.

He was already pulling himself through the window, but Ke' didn't wait. She scrambled to her feet, her body screaming in protest, and ran. She ran faster than she ever had in her life, through the dark parking lot, past rows of silent cars. She didn't know where she was going. She just ran, the night swallowing her whole.

When Terry finally dropped to the ground, panting, he was flustered, confused, and furious. He spun around, his eyes scanning the empty lot. She was gone. He had no clue which way she had gone. His entire plan, the careful, psychotic work of months, was unraveling. The shock of the realization hit him hard, and he reeled, knowing he may have just really, truly, fucked up.

But what was even more fucked up was that Terry was so caught up in pulling all this shit off, he was slipping bad. He was still in the same damn clothes that tipped Ke' off and worse, he had completely forgotten he was still wearing the sunglasses. Through the digital interface, his twin, Tory, had seen a lot and for the most part, she was all for it and extremely proud of him, but how careless he'd just gotten with Ke' was a huge problem. It wasn't a small issue that she would let slide. This was a fundamental breach of their operating procedure, and it was going to be an issue for them moving forward.

Chapter 6

"A City's Rage"

The news had started as a whisper, a flicker on a breaking news ticker, a hushed rumor passed between neighbors. Then, with the confirmation of a massive fire at Jax's estate and the chilling report of human remains uncovered, pretty soon the whispers became a profound scream. It was a roar that ripped through the city's veneer of normalcy and exposed a raw, festering wound of discontent within everyone. Everything of recent had gone from bad to worse.

Jax wasn't just a powerful man, he was the heartbeat of Lubbock. For a community that had so long been overlooked, marginalized and put down in Texas compared to its bigger cities like Houston, Dallas and San Antonio, he was an icon, an idol. He was the first Black male from within his community to actually rise up and make something of himself, and he made it his motto to stay true to his roots and used his power and platforms to create opportunities for others.

He gave away millions, funding local charities, community events, and scholarships. His label, Hub City Records, produced major hits and shined a spotlight on multiple artists worldwide, including the birth of the iconic group 3BG, led by his younger sister.

He was an architect of a fragile peace, a balance that the average citizen might not have fully understood. The news of his likely death and the brutal circumstances surrounding it, was not just a tragedy, it was a declaration of war.

The rage began in the city's heart, the ghettos. Then downtown squares, bustling marketplaces and upscale neighborhoods too. It was a low burn at first, a collective murmur of shock and disbelief that soon escalated into open defiance. People gathered in small, angry knots, their faces grim under the streetlights. They were young men and women who had grown up under Jax's protection, the mothers who believed their sons were safer because of him. For them, this wasn't just another senseless crime. This was an attack on their way of life, a direct challenge to the unspoken rules that governed their city.

Late-night protests kicked off without a leader, without a single call to action. The crowd seemed to spontaneously swell, drawn by a shared, wordless fury. They started with signs, scrawled on cardboard with thick markers, demanding answers. They wanted to know why the authorities had failed to protect one of their own. Especially one of such caliber. If he and his family weren't protected or cared for, hell, that meant everyone was fucked. The chants were simple at first, a rhythmic repetition of "Justice for Jax!" and "Who is next?"

But as the night wore on and the news anchors on television offered only carefully worded statements and vague condolences, the chants turned to shouts. The shouting became an anthem of rebellion.

The first glass window to shatter was an accident, a stray protest sign hitting a storefront. But that act, a small, inconsequential pop, was a spark in a tinderbox. The glass did more than break, it broke the spell of peaceful protest. A chorus of angry voices swelled, and the first wave of riots began to kick off. Firecrackers tossed into the streets sounded like a drumbeat of anarchy. Garbage cans were overturned, their contents spilling into the streets. Cars, their windows smashed, were left abandoned, the air thick with the smell of smoke and gasoline. The city, known for its stoic resilience, was now a portrait of a community in pain, a city on the edge.

It was more than just the death of a single man. It was the culmination of a decade of simmering frustration. The way he and his family had been picked apart one by one so brutally over the last few months, had the community feeling some kind of way, and the only way to express themselves and garner the attention and answers they deserved was to lash out.

People would lose a lot with Jax's passing, and it was absolutely devastating. It was a deep-seated fear that had been buried under the thin surface of routine life, and now it was out in the open, raw and bleeding. The city felt exposed and defenseless.

The protestors screamed at the police, their voices hoarse. They accused them of incompetence, of complicity, or just a deliberate failure to protect those who mattered most. The police, their faces grim behind their riot shields, watched as the city they were sworn to protect, tore itself apart. They were caught in the middle of a war they couldn't win, and for a terrifying moment, the city's heart seemed to stop beating, replaced by the frantic, thumping pulse of a full-blown rebellion.

The city was an inferno of rage, a canvas of fire and broken glass. It was a city that no longer recognized itself. The chaos was a physical manifestation of a collective grief, a sorrow that had nowhere to go but out, a demand for answers that had no one to answer them. It was a new beginning, a dark age now, and there was no telling how or when the city would be able to find its way back from this shit.

***

Ke's lungs burned, her legs ached, and a sharp, twisting pain shot through her stomach. She scrambled through the darkness of the hotel parking lot, the asphalt cold and unforgiving beneath her bare feet. The sounds of her own desperate sobs were drowned out by a distant roar, a deep rumble that was growing louder with every frantic step. She was running from a monster, and the only direction she could go was toward a city in chaos.

As she stumbled out onto the main street, she was hit by a wall of noise and light. The street was alive with people, a surging river of angry faces and waving signs. The air was thick with the smell of smoke, not from her brother's house, but from overturned garbage cans and smoldering tires nearby. She was surrounded by a sea of people, but she felt more alone than ever. The police, their riot gear and shields a spectacle, were being pushed back by a tide of protestors, their faces contorted with blind rage directed anywhere and seemingly everywhere.

She was an invisible ghost in the middle of it all, a woman in night clothes, her hair a wild mess, eyes wide with a terror that not too many seemed to notice. She watched a man with a tear-streaked face scream into a megaphone, his voice hoarse with grief. She saw a woman holding up a sign with a picture of Jax, the words "JUSTICE FOR JAX," written in shaky letters. They were mourning her brother, their hero, while she had just been running from the man who had likely killed him. She believed that anyway… The irony was a cold, sick weight in her stomach. Her stomach… *she thought briefly about the pregnancy…fuck!*

She didn't know what to do. She couldn't go back. She couldn't stay here. The protests were a chaotic shelter, but they offered no real protection. She was nothing more than a lost soul in the middle of a city losing its mind. She tried to blend in, to become just another face in the crowd, but her dazed eyes and her shaking body made her stand out. She was indeed as angry as all these people if not more and rightly so, but she was more so scared and in shock more than anything.

That's when she saw them. And they saw her. Two friendly looking women and a man, standing out on the edge of the protest circle, their faces filled with a recognition and concern that was different from the angry defiance of the crowd's mass. They weren't holding signs or screaming. They were simply watching her.

As she stumbled past them, they seemed to notice her, their eyes locking onto her distraught face. She must have looked like a lost child. They began to approach her, a slow, cautious movement through the chaotic throng, their expressions showing nothing but a desperate need to help a woman in need.

"Hey," the taller, lighter-skinned woman began, her voice cautious but gentle, managing to cut through the din of the protest. "You okay?"

Ke' looked at her, then back at the chaos around them, her mind blank. The woman's simple question was a far cry from the angry shouts and the breaking glass. It was a human moment in the middle of an inhuman scene, and it broke something inside her. Shaking her head, she tried to form a word, but her mouth felt dry, her throat tight.

The woman took a step closer. The other woman and the man moved in, too, forming a protective, quiet semicircle around her. "Come on," the man said softly, gesturing with his head. "Let's get you out of this mess."

They led her to a quieter spot off to the side, a shadowed corner near a storefront complex. The noise was muffled here, the chaos a distant echo. The taller woman smiled, a gesture of genuine warmth that made the tears Ke' had been fighting so hard to hold back, finally fall.

"My name's Misty," she said, her voice a calm balm. "This is my husband, Eric." Eric gave a small, fair wave, his eyes full of concern. "And this is my cousin, Syn."

Misty's expression softened. "We didn't mean to bother you, but girl, you just came out of nowhere looking like something's wrong. You're shaking, you don't have shoes on—I uh… Excuse me if I'm overstepping, but do you need help?"

A single sob escaped Ke's lips, and then another. She shook her head, unable to speak, the dam of her composure finally breaking. She cried, and she cried hard, a deep, wracking sound of grief and fear and exhaustion. The trio in front of her didn't say another word. They simply stood there, a silent wall of support, offering their presence as a shield against the world that had just fallen apart for this poor girl.

Chapter 7

"Are You Fuckin' Stupid?"

About an hour after Terry's feed suddenly cut off, the front door swung open and Terry strode in, his face lit with a victorious, arrogant grin. The heavy smell of smoke and gasoline clung to his clothes, a grim perfume of his triumph and the scent pissed Tory off.

He was humming a low tune, his shoulders back, his swagger a mirror of the confident man he had only ever pretended to be. He looked at Tory, a look of pure unadulterated pleasure on his face, expecting to be met with her approval, a hug, a glass of champagne, a blunt or something.

He didn't see the glass on the table, shattered to pieces. He didn't see the monitors, now displaying a blank screen. He didn't see the cold, murderous rage in his sister's eyes. He saw only his victory.

"Tory!" he said, his voice booming with satisfaction. "It's done, Sis. It's finally done!" He held out his arms, a gesture of shared triumph. "We got his ass! We did it!"

She didn't move.

His smile faltered. "What's wrong, T?" he asked, a flicker of confusion crossing his face. "Did you not see it? It was beautiful! That nigga had it comin', and I gave it to him!"

She took a slow, deliberate step toward him, her hands balled into fists at her sides. "Are you fucking stupid?" she said, her voice a low, dangerous whisper that cut through the silence like a knife.

Terry's grin vanished. His hands dropped to his sides, and a defensive scowl replaced his triumphant expression. "What are you talking about? What is your problem?" he demanded, his own voice rising in volume. "Everything went down exactly as I planned. That muthafucka is extra crispy right now!"

Tory's laugh was a harsh, humorless sound. "Oh, really? It went *exactly* as planned? You call what happened out there, 'the plan?'" Her eyes, usually so calm, were now two burning coals of fury. "Let's recap, shall we, since your stupid ego-tripping ass clearly missed a few things tonight."

She walked past him, her pace quick and venomous, and picked up the shattered champagne flute from the floor. She held up the broken stem, her gaze never leaving his. "First, you had to take all the credit. It wasn't 'we.' It was 'I.' You stood over Jax and grandstanded like some B-list movie villain, acting like you orchestrated this entire thing by yourself. Do you have any idea how much work went into this? The network routing jammer, the fire idea and everything else—you think you did that all by your little, lonesome self?"

Terry's face flushed. "Tory, that's not fair—"

"Shut up," she snapped. "I'm not done. You didn't allow me to go with you on this and I respected that, but when you told that nigga everything, I should have gotten some credit and a mention. Hell, Terrance was my brother too!"

She dropped the glass, the shards clattering to the floor. "Then, you had the damn audacity to drop a bomb like that on me. You're gonna be a *daddy*? You thought it was a good idea to go and impregnate the sister of the man who killed our brother? Nigga, did you really think about the logic of that? The long-term consequences? The risk? We wanted to give him a taste of his own medicine, not become a part of his fuckin' family!"

Terry opened his mouth to protest, but she cut him off again, her voice now a cold, chilling whisper. "You didn't even check the damn house before you made your move and I sat here horrified, thinking I was about to witness you die when Jax's friend almost got the jump on you. But yo' ass got lucky and I'm extremely grateful for that. One thing that really set me off though, was the fact you left a damn witness alive! That man on the steps, remember him? The man who was obviously in the house with Jax. He saw everything. The murders, the fire, the whole thing!

And you just let him go because you were too busy basking in your own twisted glory, you ain't even go the extra mile to assure there's no loose ends before you dipped. Ain't this exactly what caused us to be doing this in the first place? Literally, the exact fucking scenario, and you gone make the same damn mistake and walk in this bitch like nothing's wrong!"

She didn't wait for a response, just continued her blistering tirade. "Terry! The man you left alive... I rewound the live feed. I paused it, zoomed in on him as he screamed on the steps... And you wanna know what I saw? I saw Jax, in that man's face. The same jawline, the same set in his eyes. He wasn't just a witness to everything. He has to be his brother or something."

Tory took a step back, her voice dropping to a low, furious murmur. "News of this whole thing is traveling fast, especially on social media, and the city is in an extreme uproar over Jax's death. I've been watching since your feed cut. The thing that's both funny and yet utterly terrifying is what the reporters are saying about the remains found," she gestured at the mute tv screen. "The report says they recovered 'human remains,' singular. One set of remains. But I saw what you saw. I saw Jax go down. I saw his friend, go down. And I saw that man, Jax's brother, stuck behind a raging wall of fire. That's three people, Terry. The fire did what fires do, but it doesn't just make two whole bodies completely disappear that damn fast with no trace."

Her gaze was cold, penetrating his arrogance and finding the fear beneath. "So, let's look at this logically. Either the fire somehow completely obliterated two of the bodies and I hope somehow that's the case, or there's a serious issue. If there was just a single set of remains recovered in the entire house, then that means someone made it out. In my mind, surely Jax is dead, right? But then that means that man on the steps likely made it out, and possibly even his friend. And if they did, that is not good at all. For all we know, you left a witness alive who can identify you. Do you understand what that means? It means you've made a mess so big, so utterly fuckin' careless, that I don't know if we can clean this shit up."

Terry stood there, stunned into silence. Her words hit him like a physical blow, each one a hammer strike against his fragile sense of triumph. The look on her face wasn't just anger, it was disappointment. It was the look that told him he had failed not just her, but their very purpose.

"Now listen to me, and listen good," she said, her voice dropping to a low, authoritative growl. "This is our life. And you've just put us both in a world of hurt. From now on, you don't say 'I.' You don't make a move without running it by me first. And you don't call the shots alone. If my life or freedom is at stake, I get a say so."

And in that moment, Terry knew his victory had been an illusion, a lie he had told himself to survive. The game wasn't over. It was just getting started. And he wasn't in control of it anymore.

Tory saw the look in his eyes—the look of a man who realized he had just walked into a trap of his own making. The fury that had been boiling inside her for the last hour slowly began to cool down, replaced by the grim, methodical focus she'd always had. She took a deep breath, letting the anger settle into a hard knot in her gut. She still had his back. It was fucked up, but it was still their mission.

"Listen to me," she said, her voice calmer now, but no less serious. She walked over to him, her posture softening just enough to let him know she wasn't going to tear him apart anymore. "I know this whole situation is fucked up. Beyond fucked up. But you're still my twin. I got your back."

He didn't move, just stared at her with a daze.

"There's a lot of moving parts to all this now," she continued, her eyes scanning the blank monitors, as if she could still see the chaos on them. "And with the city coming together behind this, a lot of light is being shined on us right now, light we don't need. If we're gonna finish this how we intended, and live our best lives after, we have to do this the right way."

She paused, and her eyes, still cold, met his. "We have to go to work. We have to dig some more and find out every single hard detail about that recovery. If indeed those men made it out alive, we have to find them. And we have to kill them." She took a step closer, her voice dropping to a near whisper. "And for damn sure, we have to kill Ke'." She gave him a pointed side-eye. "I let you have your way at first and obviously, things backfired. In fact, we need to get to her first. I have a feeling if any problems were to come of this right now, they'd definitely come from her. To be real with you, we need all hands on deck with this. I say we call Bundle to fill him in and you should reach out to that detective and see if he can help somehow. We need all the help we can get."

Terry didn't like it, but he knew she was right. He knew she'd seen everything that happened at the hotel with Ke' too. He fucked up and it was no way around the obvious now. What needed to be done would be done, they had no choice. All Terry could do was shake his head and agree. When they finished talking, he pulled out his phone, put it on speaker and made a few important calls that would only pour more gas on the fire.

PART II

"Comes Around"

Chapter 8

"The Bayou's Daughter"

The descent into the basement of Big D's hideout was a nightmare in a world already turned upside down. The heavy metal door groaned on its hinges, sealing them off from the distant howl of sirens and the city's frantic chaos. The air below was thick with the smell of damp earth and stale dust, a stark contrast to the acrid stench of smoke and gasoline that still clung to them. Big D, Tyreke, and Detective Crockette moved as a single, desperate unit, their footsteps echoing in the silence as they navigated the narrow, shadowy stairs. The flashlight from Crockette's phone cut a frantic, dancing path in the gloom, illuminating the dust motes swirling in the air.

At the heart of the basement, a single, bare bulb hung from a wire, casting a weak yellow light over a large, worn-out wooden table. Without a word, the three men gently, yet urgently, laid Jax out on the cold surface. In the dim, unforgiving light, the full extent of his brokenness was on display. His face, once a picture of calm strength, was a swollen, bloody pulp. His eyes were bruised a deep ghastly purple, almost swollen shut, and his nose was visibly bent and shattered. His ribs, a series of dark, blossoming bruises, were a testament to the brutal beating he had endured. Two dark stains, already soaked through his pants, marked the twin gunshot wounds on his legs just above the knee. The blood, a thick, dark syrup, was still seeping from the torn flesh.

He should have been dead. Any normal man would have been, lying broken and battered on this table. But a shallow, almost imperceptible rise and fall of his chest was a desperate flicker of life, the only proof he still had breath in his lungs. He was on the brink, teetering between the realms of the living and the dead. As the men finally stumbled in, Angela and Tina's worry turned into a mix of shock and horror. Angela's voice, a horrified whisper, filled the silence.

"Oh my God, is he—" she began, her words catching in her throat as she stared at the unmoving body.

Crockette spoke up, his voice flat with exhaustion and a grim finality. "He's alive—barely. Not in good shape at all as you can see. Seems like he's got bruises, breaks, and multiple gunshot wounds. I know this situation is very complex, but he needs a hospital before it's too late."

"But it's never too late though, huh, D?" Tina said, something extra in her tone that prompted confusion from Tyreke, Crockette, and Angela. But Big D knew what she was hinting at. He looked at her, and his face, which had been a mask of grim determination, softened into a look of profound understanding. He knew, just as she did, that they were about to dive into a world that neither of the others could comprehend. The two of them had never spoken of it before, a mutual, unspoken pact to leave the past where it belonged. But now with Jax's life hanging in the balance, that pact was now broken.

Tyreke, still reeling from the chaos of the night, looked from Tina to Big D. "What you talkin' bout?" he demanded, his voice laced with confusion and fear. "What's not too late? He's dying, we need a doctor!" A moment of silence passed amongst everyone before Tyreke spoke again. "So, what the fuck? Someone gone do something, say something or something or we just gone watch my brother die on this rotten ass table?"

Tina, her face pale but her eyes burning with a cold, steady resolve, finally turned to Tyreke. "Jax isn't going to die, but the physical damage done to his body is something that will cause him much pain and who knows what kind of side effects down the road if we don't do something right now. I really don't want to go this route, God knows I don't! But at this point we don't really have a choice. Now, in order for me to do this and do this right, I need two things," she said, looking more at Big D than anyone else.

"What do you need?" Angela asked, her anxiety high.

"I need a phone, please tell me y'all have one." She looked at Crockette and Tyreke, her eyes urgent.

Crockette, without a word, unlocked his phone and handed it to her. Tina took it and, with a firm, low voice that brooked no argument, laid out her last command. "I need y'all to stay back and stay quiet."

Tina took a deep breath and dialed a number she hadn't called in years, but the ten digits were forever cemented into her memory. In two short rings, her call was answered, almost as if the call was anticipated and the one answering was expecting this very moment.

***

A voice answered, rich and heavy with an unmistakable southern drawl, like molasses, poured slowly over a drumbeat. *"Hello, my child. I was expecting your call. I could feel it."*

The words weren't loud, but they carried, filling every shadowy corner of the basement. The sound slithered out of the phone speaker, wrapping around them, chilling bone and soul alike.

Angela gasped softly. Tyreke flinched. Even Crockette— stone-faced, sharp-eyed Crockette—felt the hair rise on the back of his neck.

He raised his eyebrows, finally giving voice to the unease they all shared. "That's a private number you just dialed from. She answered like she knew… and you didn't even say a word yet. How the hell—"

Before Tina could open her mouth, the voice on the phone cut in, smooth and certain.

"I know lots of things, Brandon."

Crockette froze. He hadn't introduced himself. He hadn't even spoken his full name since he'd stepped into this hell of a night. But the way she said it, sharp and sure, told him this wasn't luck, or chance, or guessing.

"I have lots of feelings." Madam Linda's tone shifted then, layered with something deeper, older. It was like she was speaking from underwater, or from a room just behind their reality. "And I feel your doubt, Detective. I feel your questions. I feel the sweat in the palm of your hand as you reach for that gun you keep tucked too close to your ribs. But that won't help you now."

Silence.

Jax groaned faintly on the table, his body trembling with the effort of simply being alive. The sound snapped everyone back into the moment, but none of them looked away from the phone in Tina's hand.

Big D was the only one unfazed. He had leaned back against the wall, arms crossed, his eyes heavy but certain. He'd known. He'd always known.

Tina's voice cracked when she finally spoke, softly and reverently, like a daughter admitting weakness. "Mama… he's dyin'. I-I didn't want to call, but I don't have nowhere else to turn."

On the other end of the line, a low chuckle rumbled, not cruel, but carrying centuries of knowing. *"Death is always close, my baby. He walk with us from the first cry. But tonight… Tonight he been tricked. Pulled away too soon, your boy, and now he lost between the doors. We can fix that. But you know what it means."*

The room seemed to grow colder. Angela rubbed her arms, shivering as though a draft had crept in, though the basement air was still. Tyreke muttered under his breath, "What the fuck..." but didn't finish the thought.

Crockette narrowed his eyes. "What the hell does she mean, Tina? What's she talking about?"

Tina's eyes welled with tears she fought to keep from falling. She couldn't look at him. She couldn't look at any of them. Instead, she stared at Jax's battered face, his shallow breaths rattling like a whisper of goodbye.

"Y'all wanted to save him," she said hoarsely. "This is the only way."

The voice on the line dipped low, both tender and commanding. *"First, you have to open yourself, my baby. You don't need to believe, not like I do. But you must allow me to pass through you, to use your tongue, your hands. That's the only way. The spirits won't answer me from here unless they hear my voice through blood that's mine."*

Tina's jaw clenched. "I don't... I don't follow them ways, Mama. I never wanted this life. I ain't never wanted to be like you."

There was a pause on the line, and for the first time, a faint sadness colored Linda's words. *"I know, child. I never forced it. But right now, belief don't matter. Choice don't matter. Only Jax's breath matters. You want to save him? Then let me through."*

The group exchanged uneasy glances.

Crockette shifted uncomfortably, shaking his head. "This is crazy. She's talking about possession, Tina. You really gonna—"

"Shut the fuck up," Tyreke snapped, his voice cracking with desperation. "Look at him! My brother dyin' right in front of us and you worried about crazy? I don't care what it is—if it saves him, I'm with it." His wide eyes darted to Tina, pleading. "Please. Do it. Shit, if not I will, give me the damn phone and tell me what to do!"

Angela, hugging herself, whispered, "But what if it's not him anymore when it's done? What if it changes him?" She didn't sound like she was asking anyone in particular.

Big D stayed still, his arms folded across his chest, his gaze steady on Tina. He didn't offer comfort, didn't speak doubt. He simply nodded once, slow, like he'd already accepted whatever came next.

Tina looked around the room — at Crockette's skeptical glare, Tyreke's terror, Angela's trembling, Big D's silence. Finally, she lowered her head. "Fine. I'll do it. But hear me, Mama—I ain't converting. I ain't carryin' on your ways after this. I'm just… borrowing 'em for tonight."

The laugh that came through the phone wasn't mocking. It was warm, proud, tinged with something ancient. *That's all I ask."*

The phone crackled, and then Madam Linda's voice changed. It grew heavier, like it carried centuries, the sound thick with words almost too old to exist. A chant spilled out, the syllables curling strange in Tina's ears, half-familiar and half-unintelligible.

Her own lips began to move, trembling at first, then steadying, until the chant was pouring from her mouth. She didn't recognize the language, couldn't place the sound, but the syllables rode her breath anyway, flowing like water pulled by gravity.

Crockette's eyes widened. "She… she's not even saying that herself," he muttered, stepping back. "It's like the words are using her."

The basement shifted. The air grew heavier, pressing down on their shoulders. The single bulb overhead flickered, buzzing like a trapped wasp. Angela gasped, clutching her chest, swearing she heard whispering in the walls. Tyreke staggered back, shaking his head violently as if the sounds were crawling inside his skull.

Through it all, Big D stood unmoving, watching Tina transform into a vessel for something greater than herself.

The chant ended with a sharp, guttural sound, and then silence. Tina's body slumped slightly, sweat beading on her brow. Her eyes fluttered, then snapped open—but the voice that came out wasn't hers.

"Now… lay him bare."

The command echoed, layered with her mother's accent and something deeper, something that made Crockette's skin crawl.

Tina's hands, steady now, reached down. With a strange calm, she began to strip Jax of his ruined clothes. Shirt, torn and bloodied, peeled away. Pants cut carefully to expose the bullet wounds. Every mark, every bruise, every break was revealed under the pale-yellow light, his broken body bared for the ritual.

Angela turned away, unable to watch. Tyreke pressed a fist to his mouth, tears welling as his brother's wounds lay raw before them.

The phone, still on speaker, hissed with static like the sound of cicadas in a swamp. Then Madam Linda's voice came again, low and satisfied. *"Good. Now the spirits can see where he hurt. Now they can decide if he worth savin'."*

The air pulsed heavy with expectation. The bulb flickered once more, then held steady, its glow stretched thin.

Then came the final decree, rolling through Tina's lips with absolute finality. *"You must leave him be. Helping in't for your eyes to see. Cover him whole with a sheet until sunrise and don't peek. When he rises again, he will be like new."*

The words struck like a hammer in the silence. Angela's hand shot to her mouth, muffling a sob. Tyreke's eyes went wide, torn between hope and fear.

Crockette shook his head slowly, his skepticism at war with the shiver running down his spine.

Big D, his expression unreadable, moved first. Without speaking, he dragged a clean sheet from the corner and handed it to Tina. She unfolded it with trembling hands and laid it gently over Jax's broken frame, tucking it around him like a shroud.

The bulb above them flickered once more, humming as if in protest, then steadied into a weak but constant glow. The basement seemed to exhale, a long, low sigh that none of them could explain.

Madam Linda's presence faded from Tina's body as quickly as it came. Her shoulders sagged, her lips stilled and when her eyes lifted, they were her own again, wet with tears and rimmed with exhaustion.

No one spoke. No one dared.

Chapter 9

"Next of Kin"

Ke' was still on the curb, knees pulled tight to her chest, when the last of her cries finally broke into hiccupped breaths. Misty stayed crouched beside her, rubbing slow circles on her back while Eric and Syn hovered close, exchanging looks that said they weren't sure what had just fallen into their laps. When Ke' finally lifted her face, streaked with tears and damp hair sticking to her cheeks, she whispered, "Thank y'all."

"No problem," Misty said quickly, her tone gentle but firm, like she was trying to anchor Ke' back to solid ground. Eric gave a nod of agreement while Syn folded her arms, her eyes sharp but not unkind.

"Listen," Misty continued, "we're not about to leave you sitting out here like this. If you need a ride, or to call somebody, we got you. Whatever you need."

Ke' shook her head faintly, not in refusal but in the hollow way of someone too drained to decide. The vagueness made Misty's brow knit, her instinct telling her this girl carried more than just tears. Syn caught it too, the edge of suspicion narrowing her gaze.

It was Eric who finally broke the silence. "Come on," he said, steady but calm. "Ain't no sense stayin' out here in the open. Let's get in the car, at least. Figure things out as we go. They ain't letting up round here no time soon, probably get worse if anything."

Ke' hesitated, glancing from one face to the next, but something in their mix—Misty's warmth, Eric's steadiness, even Syn's hard honesty—made her nod. Slowly, with Misty's hand still steadying her, she rose to her feet and followed them.

Moments later, Ke' was curled in the back seat of their sedan, the world sliding by in streaks of neon and shadow as the night carried her someplace she couldn't yet name.

Her tears had finally slowed, drying sticky on her cheeks, leaving her drained but strangely lighter, as though the weight she carried had cracked open for the first time.

Misty, sitting beside her, leaned close but careful not to crowd. "Hey… hey, it's alright now. You're safe, okay? Just breathe."

Her voice was warm, the kind you didn't have to believe in order for it to help. In the front seat, Eric kept glancing back at her in the rearview mirror, concern cutting deep into his sharp features. Syn, riding shotgun, didn't say much at first. But unlike Misty's gentle comfort, Syn's silence carried an edge—like she was watching everything, waiting for the first sign that this stranger might break apart all over again.

Ke' wiped her face with the back of her sleeve, trying to put herself back together. "Thank y'all," she whispered again, her voice barely audible over the hum of the tires on the cracked asphalt. "For stopping. For helping."

"It's really no problem," Eric said, his tone even, not the kind to make a big deal out of something decent. "Anybody would've done the same."

Syn gave a short laugh, dry and low. "Don't kid her, D. Most folks wouldn't have slowed down, let alone opened the door. You're lucky it was us, girl."

Misty shot Syn a quick look. "You don't gotta scare her."

"I ain't scarin' her," Syn said, turning slightly in her seat, her sharp eyes cutting to Ke'. "I'm keepin' it real. World out here's cold. You picked the right strangers to cry in front of, that's all."

Ke' managed a weak nod. "Still... thank you."

Misty softened, squeezing Ke's hand. "Listen, we can take you wherever you need to go. Or, if you want us to call somebody for you, we'll wait. Just... let us know what you need."

Ke' shook her head, more to herself than at them. Her lips trembled before she still forced them. "I... I don't know yet."

The answer was too vague, too clipped, and Misty caught it. She tilted her head, curiosity sparking. "Okay. Well, you don't got to know right now. But if there's something...anything...we can do, we're not just gonna drop you off on a corner and drive away."

Syn leaned back against the seat, arms crossed, still watching Ke' like she was trying to read a language only she understood.

Ke' didn't respond right away. She stared out the window, watching the streetlights flicker past, the glow sliding across her face like ghosts. Finally, she breathed out, low and shaky. "I've been runnin' a long time..."

"Running? Running from who and for what?" Eric asked.

"Running from the man I think might've killed my brother..."

"Oh, my Go—" Misty started, but Syn cut in, her tone sharp and demanding.

"Killed your brother? Who is your brother?" Syn threw in and turned fully in her seat. She was all ears for this. Ke's words were enough to make Eric slam the brakes. The car lurched violently, tires screeching against the wet asphalt. A horn blared behind them as headlights swerved, the driver whipping past with a spray of water and a furious yell swallowed by the night.

Ke's throat barely worked, dry as dust, but she forced herself to nod and speak. "Yeah... I'm Ke' Cook."

The air in the car changed, heavy with the weight of her words. Syn was the first to break it, wide-eyed, then letting out a nervous laugh that had just a little too much edge. "Aw, shit… I got warrants." She leaned back in her seat like the cops might materialize out of thin air just for being this close to Ke'.

Misty's hand flew out in a sharp wave, cutting the thought before it grew. "Bitch, ain't nobody worried about your old-ass tickets." Her voice had bite, but it carried a dismissive humor, her focus snapping right back to Ke'. She twisted in her seat, eyes locking on the girl with sudden urgency. "Girl, wait—what? Help me understand. How you end up here, like this? What happened?"

Before Ke' could gather an answer, Eric shifted in the driver's seat, his movements deliberate. He tugged the slim earpiece from his ear, the faint static cutting off as he set it aside. Then, with a quick tap on the dash, he twisted the volume knob until the car filled with the low murmur of a news broadcast bleeding through the speakers. "Look," Eric said, voice steady but grim. "Listen to this."

***

The anchor's voice was crisp, professional, yet heavy with the gravity of her report. *"…Authorities in Lubbock County are on edge tonight as the city reels from yet another tragedy. The fire at the White estate has left many believing that beloved icon Jax White is dead. For many residents, this loss marks the final blow—the straw that broke the camel's back. Citizens are demanding answers, furious over the string of violence tied to this family that has played out in plain view of the entire city.*

Let's recall… the murders of Jax's closest friends at a city nightclub… the police shooting of his younger brother, promising athlete Marcus Cook… the bombing that took the life of his sister, Kam—leader of the global music group 3BG… the latter revealed the prolonged poisoning death of his mother, Mecia Cook… and now, Jax himself.

Tonight, police are warning the public that these are not isolated incidents. They say the obvious pattern cannot be ignored. And yet, as officials speak, questions continue to mount. The latest twist: Lubbock County Police are now asking for the city's help in locating an individual closely connected to these tragedies. Her name is Ke' Cook— believed to be the youngest sister of Jax White and the last surviving member of the Cook-White family as we know it.

Authorities are torn about how to view her role. On one hand, Ke' is listed as next of kin, presumed to be enduring unimaginable loss. But on the other, as Police Chief Doyle said earlier tonight, 'Either this Ke' Cook girl is truly enduring unfortunate tragedies in her life right now, and indeed should be worried, 'cause she may be targeted next in what seems to be a dangerous pattern... Or—and I hope this is not the case—she may be involved somehow, some way, or knows something. Either way, she's connected to this and needs to talk with us.'

Adding to the tension, sources confirm that since the bombing of the Lubbock Police Department precinct, the force has been short-staffed and stretched thin. With violence spiking, there are whispers of the city moving toward a full-scale lockdown—martial law measures that could bring dozens of FBI investigators and National Guard units into the streets, setting curfews and checkpoints until order is restored.

While officials have not yet confirmed, those close to the situation say announcements could come within days. Authorities emphasize that every move is being scrutinized. Rumors swirl that city officials are considering further restrictions and a partial lockdown, before week's end. Residents are being urged to remain indoors where possible, and officials warn that any public gatherings may be prohibited until further notice.

Meanwhile, law enforcement sources continue to stress that locating Ke' Cook is critical—not only because she is the next of kin to Jax White, but also because she may hold information vital to understanding the sequence of attacks that have plagued and damaged this city. This is a city on edge, watching history unfold in the streets it calls home. It has now reached a point where every citizen must ask, can anyone be safe, and will justice finally be served?"

***

Ke' swallowed, throat tight, the weight of her own name broadcast into every living room and car in Lubbock County, pressing down like concrete. Her hands clenched in her lap. "I... I didn't... I didn't know... it was this bad," she murmured, voice barely audible.

Every single person in the car was born and raised in Lubbock, Texas, the eastside to be exact. Jax White's story was something they all knew all too well. Eric admired the man's grit and ultimate success. Hell, they were all fans of Hub City Records. Syn had been a devoted follower of Kam and 3BG, the global girl group she led. Misty's mother had gone to the same church as Mecia Cook, often speaking of her and the family.

They were all aware of the tragedies that had rocked the city in recent weeks, which was why they had been out at the protest in the first place. But none of them could have imagined they were about to come this close to the truth— rooted in a reality far bigger, more dangerous, than anything they'd ever faced.

Eric was loyal to Misty, and that loyalty ran deep. He trusted her instincts implicitly. Now, seeing what was unfolding, he found himself genuinely interested, alert but not scared. Misty, with her big heart, was naturally committed to helping anyone in need, no matter the scenario. She couldn't walk away from a situation like this. And as for Syn—well, she wasn't one to back down. Shit, she was down for whatever was about to take place from here.

Together, they made an uneasy but determined group, each processing the gravity of the news in their own way, each bracing for whatever came next.

Chapter 10

"Questions & Answers"

Big D, Tyreke, Tina, Angela, and Detective Crockette followed Madam Linda's orders, leaving Jax alone in the basement. Each step up the narrow, creaking stairs felt heavier than the last, their minds spinning with everything they had just witnessed.

When they finally emerged into the night, the cool air hit them like a wave. They found themselves on the abandoned family farmland, shadows stretching long under the dim glow of the moon. For a moment, they all breathed a little easier—free for just a second—but the relief was shallow. The stress hadn't dissipated. The worry about Jax's condition, and the uncertainty of what lay ahead for everyone, lingered like a storm cloud ready to break at a moment's notice.

Everybody had questions, and everyone wanted answers. "Now surely, I'm not the only one who wants to know what the fuck is up?" Tyreke let off, his voice raw with frustration as it cracked through the night air.

He dragged a hand down his face, pacing in the dirt, then snapped back toward the group. "I think I speak for everybody when I say this shit is way too real and far too deep to be in and not know or understand what's happening here. I know I don't know y'all well and y'all don't know me, but somehow, we all in this shit together now. Somebody gon' have to talk to me... 'cause this shit is crazy." Tyreke's words hung heavy in the night, the silence pressing on them like a weight.

"I agree," Detective Crockette added, his voice low but firm. "Don't look like we'll be leavin' anytime soon given the circumstances. I think it's about time we all have ourselves a little Q and A."

"Q and A?" Tina echoed, her brows furrowed, confusion flashing across her tired face.

Angela sighed, her voice soft but steady as she filled in the gap. "Questions and answers," she explained, glancing around at the others. "And I think he's right. We need to put it all on the table. Now."

"Damn straight we do," Tyreke said, his voice cutting through the dark like a blade. "Cause so far, nothin' I've seen tonight makes sense." He shifted his weight, his eyes narrowing as they landed squarely on Big D. The big man stood quiet, arms crossed, face carved from stone, but his silence spoke louder than words.

"Yeah, D... how 'bout we start with you, huh?" Tina shot at him, her tone sharp but trembling underneath. "Help us understand what could have happened to bring us here like this."

All eyes turned to Big D. The night air felt heavier, the silence stretching out until it was almost unbearable. The big man shifted, jaw tight, shoulders rising and falling with a slow breath, but still he said nothing.

"C'mon now, it's obvious—at least to me," Tina snapped, voice breaking with frustration. "You and my mother been had something cooked up long before tonight, D! Don't play with me. I saw the damn tape from the feed, how you went through that fire, and we all just saw what we had to do to Jax just now. What the fuck is going on? Tell me the truth!" The fire in Tina's eyes left no room for sidestepping.

"Look... I ain't got all the answers, a'ight? If I knew half of this shit, we wouldn't be out here in the first damn place... You think I planned any of this? Knew it was gonna go down like this? Hell no… I'm just as lost as y'all on that. I don't know why any of this shit started… who's behind any of it," Big D admitted, shoulders slumping slightly, voice low. "All I know is we in it now, and so far, I've done everything I can to help. And I ain't stoppin'. I'll keep doin' it."

"I wanna know… how long, D?" Tina demanded, eyes burning.

"How long what?"

"How long since you made that damn pact with my mother, huh? Yeah, there's a lot that needs to be discussed, but answer that… it'll put a lot into perspective for me."

Big D knew exactly what Tina was hinting at, and he knew it had to be addressed. It wasn't exactly the ideal place for a conversation like this, but given everything that had just gone down, he couldn't honestly say it was the wrong time either.

"The deal I made with your mother all those years ago…It wasn't what you think. It had nothing to do with tonight or what happened to my family. Seeing where I'm at now, all this… Shit, I can say I'm glad I did it. I just wish it had worked for everyone."

Big D looked at all their eyes on him. Everyone was tuned in, wanting to hear it all. He was never the kind of man to oblige to such demands, but given the depth of everything, he chose to relent and give them what they wanted.

"Back in my day, when I was out here doing my thing in all my glory, doing deals, doing dirt, building my name while playing the game, I reached a point where I thought I knew it all and had all the power. I knew the only thing that could ever stop me and what I wanted to accomplish was *death*," he paused.

"Every man is destined for something… sometimes destined for things far beyond rational understanding," he continued, letting the weight of the words settle.

Tina interjected sharply. "But wait, wait—I never even introduced you to my mother officially. I mean, I told you some things, but it doesn't make sense how you two did this, or really why you still did it."

"Yes," he replied, "I'll explain. See basically, this all started in the late nineties. One day I was at this gas station in the hood, and seen this bad lil chick I never seen before, looking like she was flagging niggas down or trying to, but not havin' much luck even though she was fine as hell. I approached her and she automatically pegged me for a trick, but she just ain't know—"

Before he could go into detail about how they met, Tina cut him off. "Nigga, I remember how we met. Fuck all that. Don't get cute. Get to the point."

Big D nodded. "That part was important but fuck it, fast forward two years later… One day, business called for me to go to Louisiana to meet with a new potential business partner. And a crazy thing happened—something similar to tonight—except I received a mysterious call from a voice all too identical to the one we just heard. The lady knew me and knew things about me that no one should.

It was one of the only things in my life up to that point that truly scared me, but it intrigued me as well. She gave me instructions and directions on where to meet. And well… I went." He leaned against the old house slightly, letting the silence stretch around his words. "When I made it to the dock out in the swampy waters, I stepped on like she asked me to, and I waited in the fog as I listened to all the sounds of the night."

The cool air held them tight, every eye on Big D as he paused and drew a slow breath, anticipating the story ahead.

"I waited patiently on that dock for a while before I started to second guess myself and just leave. The moment I decided I was going to step off, the dock started to move… on its own. Damn near scared the shit out of me. It floated me across the river lazily, and when I reached the other side of the dark waters, I was face-to-face with a crooked cabin, shrouded in a curtain of mist. When I approached the cabin door, it opened wide with no one on the other side, and I stopped dead in my tracks. But that familiar voice called me forward.

I crossed the threshold of the doorway, and I felt an energy unlike anything I'd ever felt. But I brushed it off and crept forward, then the door shut on its own right behind me. A warm glow from down the hall caught my eye and the energy pulled me in that direction. I walked down that hallway and it was like entering another realm, an unreal place, yet it was very real.

No lie—it was some real spooky shit in that house—to this day I can't explain or comprehend fully, and I can say the only reason I showed up there in the first place was like a compulsion. It's like I was drawn there by an invisible force or something. The need to know who this person was, how she had such knowledge—it drove me…So I entered a large room at the back of the place, parting a curtain of hanging beads that rattled softly as I stepped through.

The air inside was thick with smoke and strange scents— sage, incense, something older I couldn't name. The walls were lined with dusty shelves stacked with jars, bones, worn candles, and books that looked centuries old. It was the kind of room you'd expect out of some story whispered about down South, the kind of room that made the hairs on your arm stand up because you knew things had happened there— real things.

And that's when I saw her. *Madam Linda.* Seated at a table carved with symbols I didn't understand, eyes fixed on me like she'd been waiting all along. Her voice came steady, rich, and commanding as she raised one of those long, gnarled fingers toward the bench across from her. *"Come, my children... sit."* Big D let those words hang heavy in the night air, his deep voice low as he recalled them.

"My *children?*" Tina's eyes narrowed, her body jerking forward like she'd caught something the others missed. "Wait—hold on. What do you mean by that, D?"

The big man exhaled slowly, his shoulders sinking as he nodded. "Yeah… I wasn't alone that night actually." Everyone's faces tightened, confusion and disbelief flashing across their eyes. "I had Jax with me."

"Nigga, what?" Tina's voice cracked like a whip. The group froze, shock rippling through them all at once. "You took a damn child with you? A kid!"

Big D's tone stayed calm, but the weight of his words pressed on everyone. "Listen… I never had kids of my own. Back in those days, my nephew Jax was my everything. I had big dreams for him, for my family. We were close. At that time, he was five, maybe six… still young, still impressionable. I took him on that road trip partly just to spend time with him, like I always did back then, but also because it made sense in my line of work." He glanced around, meeting each of their stunned faces.

For a long beat, no one spoke. The words hung in the air like a blade over their heads. Angela's voice cracked, her eyes wide with disbelief. "You took Jax—*little Jax*—into something like that?"

Tina's eyes burned hotter than all of them. She stepped forward, trembling with a mix of fury and confusion. "All this time, D. All this time, you held that back? And got the nerve to act like we just supposed to be okay with it?"

Big D didn't flinch at her fire, but the weight of their judgment pressed on him. He stood still, chest rising and falling slow, his silence louder than their voices until the noise died down.

When he finally spoke, his tone was heavy, steady, and raw. "In my world, moving with a kid gave me cover. People see a man with a child, they don't second-guess him, don't look too hard. It was insurance, a way to move freer. Yeah, I know—you could call it reckless, dangerous even. But you gotta understand, I wasn't thinkin' rational back then. I was driven. Pulled by something I didn't understand. That's the only reason he was there. So, all you muthafuckas can miss me with the judgment, a'ight? If I had not made the choice I made, shit there's a very good chance Jax would be dead right now and shit, me too. I would have surely met my end a long time ago."

The words hit the ground between them like a brick, and nobody moved. Angela wrapped her arms around herself, her eyes darting away from Big D like she couldn't stand looking at him in the moment. Detective Crockette shifted, lips pressed thin, but even he didn't speak. Tyreke muttered under his breath, pacing in tight circles before finally stopping, hands on his hips, staring at the dirt like the answers might be written there.

The silence stretched so long it almost felt like another presence had stepped into the circle with them. It was thick, heavy, suffocating. Everyone seemed to be waiting for someone else to break it.

Finally, Tina did. "Alright… fine. You took him there. But that still don't tell me what really went down." Her eyes locked on Big D, burning hot but sharper now, like she was cutting straight through every excuse he had left. She stepped closer, fists trembling at her sides. "You talkin' about *my mother* here, D. Don't play with me. I know it's more to the story." Her words hit like knives, each one deliberate. Her breath caught, and her voice rose, heavy with accusation. "What did she do to you, D?"

Big D looked at her, "I know this gon' sound crazy and unbelievable to you, considerin' the things you know or assume about your mother and the heritage you come from," he said, voice rough and careful. "But this ain't what you think. I took on no commitments. I owe no debts. There's no ties. That woman didn't do anything to me—truly. What she did was give me a gift, one unlike anything I'd ever received… Before that night, I didn't know her personally. But apparently, she'd been watching me for years. She knew I was the one responsible for pulling you, the person she loved most, out of situations she didn't agree with—or have

87

the power to fix. It was me who saved you, Tina. Provided for you. Protected you. And for that… she gave me this *gift*."

While he had their undivided attention, he continued. "That night the air was thick with smoke and incense. Candles burned in holders carved with symbols I didn't understand. Salt lined the floors in circles and patterns. She had us sit—me and Jax—at her table, her eyes boring into mine. She didn't need to ask if I loved you. She knew. She knew everything. She appreciated the loyalty I showed, how I protected you when she couldn't. And in return, she offered something that would assure your protection, your safety, and help me protect my family and my business and build a real legacy. A simple gesture in her eyes, but with unimaginable potential in mine."

He could see the questions forming on their faces. "She performed a ritual," he began, voice low, deliberate. "She didn't just wave her hands or mutter some words—every detail was intentional. The room… it was alive with energy. Candles flickered in precise patterns, smoke curling in spirals above the salt-lined floor. Herbs burned in a circle around us, their scent thick and sharp, cutting through the air. She had us sit on the floor, knees bent, palms open. Her eyes didn't leave mine. It was like she was reading the very core of me, seeing every thought, every intent. She touched us, not roughly, but with a pressure that made me feel every nerve in my body hum. She spoke in a language I didn't understand, yet I felt every word inside me.

And when it was all done… when she finally stepped back, I could feel it in my bones—we were different. The gist of it, the way I understand it now, is *physical immortality*. We are human in every way—feel pain, bleed, get hurt—but the only way we can actually die is if our heart or head is taken from the body whole. That's it. Otherwise… we endure. We survive. We overcome—or we suffer indefinitely. For me, she foresaw fire in my future—destruction, chaos. She gave me a shield of sorts, something to repel it, to walk through flames and survive when any normal man would fall.

And Jax... she saw him endure the night without crying, without complaint, showing strength beyond his years. She marked him, in a way. Told me he would always be a winner, that to beat him, one would have to cheat. He carries her favor, subtle but unbreakable, like a current running beneath his life. The only thing she asked for in return is that we lived, continue life as normal, and never speak of the moment. Of course, I never said a word until now. And Jax... well, he was so young, I'm sure he doesn't remember it all. But there's your truth."

"So that's it... that explains how I got so lucky and only a part of my body looks like this," Tina said as she raised her shirt, revealing her burn scar she tried to hide with the intricate dragon tattoo blowing flames toward the charred skin.

Big D's eyes softened, taking in the sight of the scar she had carried all these years, hidden in plain sight beneath her art. "So that's what you really were after, huh," he said quietly, his voice low but steady, "Yes, T. That's how you made it out of that house and Dre didn't. Even though you did what you did, I saved you. That's what hurt me back then and made me cut you off, and we know what happened after that..." Big D admitted.

Tina's hands trembled slightly as she traced the edges of the dragon's tail curling around the burn. "I never... I never understood how I survived, why I wasn't—" her voice caught. "To make sense of things I assumed something way different but, in my gut, I always knew...especially after that whole court incident I knew it. Dammit, I knew."

Detective Crockette and Tyreke were lost, but for the most part, Angela was clued in. She and Tina had been talking for years and things came up that all made sense in the grand scheme of things now that the bigger was forming in real time.

"Uh, I don't know if it's just me, but I was with ya' till the end and you lost me," Tyreke stated.

"Nah, I'm with you on that one," the detective added.

"Weird as it is, bottom line—Jax isn't dying and he will be okay, just like Madam Linda said, come sunrise," Big D made it clear. "Now what we need to focus on is figuring out exactly who caused all this shit by sunrise, and what we are gonna do about it. That's the number one question I want the answer to!"

"Well, I have the answer to that question or at least half an answer," Tyreke disclosed with all eyes on him now. The energy and spotlight shifted for fifteen minutes.

"Every bit of information is vital at this point... let's hear it," Angela welcomed his words.

Tyreke looked worried about what he was about to say next. He didn't want to add more bullshit to the astronomical amount of bullshit they were already going through. Tina saw it all over his face. "It's okay, we've heard so much tonight, and seen so much recently, I mean... how much worse can it be?"

Tyreke ran a hand through his hair, pacing in the dirt again. "I... I don't even know why this is happening," he admitted. "That's what's killing me the most right now. But... I got this gut feeling that the person who tried to kill Jax... it's someone close. Someone in the family. One of our cousins."

"Cousin!" Big D's voice full, disbelief and shock cutting through the night. He stepped closer, brow furrowed. "Hold up, Tyreke. You serious right now?"

"I'm serious," Tyreke said, stopping mid-step and turning toward them. "I don't know exactly why, but the guy I saw in the mansion... he looked exactly like one of our cousins. A cousin I've never even met in person before. I only seen 'em in a few old family photos my dad had. He was really young in the photos, but he has the same baby face and features. Of course he's aged, obviously, but when I pictured his face again when I saw him leaving the mansion, it hit me like… *he looks a hell of a lot like my uncle Andre.*

According to my pops, Uncle Andre had three kids. Two boys and one girl. I met the oldest boy Terrance by chance once at a sporting event back in middle school days. We are close in age and we talked sometimes, even did business a time or two when we got older, but that's it. Said the youngest two kids were twins, a boy and a girl and I remember their names start with a T, but I can't recall the actual names."

Big D's jaw dropped. He glanced at Tina, certain details of the recent past dancing through his brain. He stared at Tyreke, the weight of the revelation sinking in. "Wait a minute… you're tellin' me… this cousin, this guy—if he's who you think he is—that means..." His voice trailed off, realization dawning slowly.

Big D rubbed his face slowly, eyes scanning the moonlit horizon. "Damn… damn. This… this just got way bigger. Way crazier. Way more fucked up then I thought. I thought I'd seen it all, … but this—this is a whole different level. And if he's involved… that means this mess, this whole thing has ties to both our pasts. All this shit that has happened could have very well be my fault."

Angela and Tina exchanged uneasy glances, sensing the tension and the weight of the connections forming before them. Detective Crockette silently processed the implications.

Big D's eyes narrowed as the pieces started to shift in his head. He looked straight at Tyreke. "Okay, so let me get this straight… Tyreke—you're Jax's half-brother. Through your father… Mar. As in Marcellus White, right?"

Tyreke shifted uncomfortably, rubbing the back of his neck. "Yes. I mean… we literally just met, but I've had knowledge of him my whole life. It's just—there was some kind of situation between my pops and Jax's mom, which is why we never saw each other. He came down to meet us when she passed, and I guess she told Jax a few things about Dad. After that, we met up, wanted to spend some time together, you know... get to know each other." He let the weight of it settle, then shook his head, almost in disbelief. "And then all this shit happened."

Tyreke's eyes cut back to Big D, curiosity sharpening his tone. "But you... you asked me that so casually. Do you know my father or somethin'?"

Big D leaned back a little, eyes narrowing on Tyreke like he was measuring every word that came out of his mouth. "Oh, I definitely know your father," he said, his tone firm but even. "Me and ole' Chucc Rucc go way back—longer than you probably realize. But right now, we gotta keep things on track." He shifted his weight forward, voice tightening. "So, let me get this straight—Marcellus is your pops, right? And he's got a brother named Andre..." Big D paused, his jaw tightening as he spoke the name. "This Andre nigga... where's he from?"

Tyreke shrugged, looking uneasy. "Uh... to be honest with you, I'm not sure. I never officially met the nigga either. But, me and the rest of my siblings, we're from Odessa. Dad moved there from Lubbock back in the day, so I would assume he's from there too. Why you askin'?"

Big D leaned in, eyes sharp. "Well, answer me this—are Andre and your dad full brothers? Same parents, same last name?"

Tyreke shook his head. "Nah. They are half-brothers. Same dad—my grandpa Michael Price. But my dad got his mama's last name, that's why all of us carry White. I assume Andre got his mama's last name."

Big D's tone cut deeper. "What makes you so sure?"

Tyreke rubbed his chin, searching his memory. "Well... 'cause on the few photographs I seen, on the back it was signed as Andre—or sometimes just Dre' Carter."

The moment that name hit the air, Big D froze. That was the confirmation he'd been fishing for. His jaw tightened, nostrils flaring. He didn't say a word, but the look on his face said it all—*Fuck!*

Across from him, Tina's eyes went wide, her heart skipping. The name *Carter* meant something to her too, pieces shifting and locking into place in her mind that she hadn't dared put together before.

The air grew heavier, silence pressing on the group as if the name itself carried weight none of them were ready for.

Tyreke looked around, reading the sudden shift in everybody's faces—the tension, the silence, the way Tina's eyes had gone wide and Big D's jaw locked tight. "Um… okay," he said slowly, scanning the group. "What the fuck was that about? Clearly y'all know something I don't."

Angela and Detective Crockette were silent, just watching the trio's exchange in front of them. The conversation slowed to a halt prompting someone to keep things rolling. Angela casually glanced between Big D and Tina before finally speaking up. "Yeah… you two look like you just saw a ghost. What's this really about?"

Detective Crockette narrowed his eyes, his tone sharper, more demanding. "Spit it out. If that name means somethin' now's the time to say it. No more holdin' back."

At this point Big D looked like he was ready to hand the floor over to Tina, to give her the chance to say whatever she needed to say. But the look in her eyes told him everything, she wasn't up for it. The memory was too raw, the truth still too close to the skin. So, the burden fell back on him. He took a long, steadying breath, shoulders rising and falling like a man bracing to lift something heavy.

"Okay," he began, voice low and deliberate. "So, with everything that's been happening to my family lately, I been tryin' to piece together what coulda sparked all this. With the info we've collected since this shit started, and the new shit that Tyreke just put on the table, I think I might got a line on why somebody would come after Jax. Now I ain't sayin' I'm one-hundred percent sure—hell, I'm not—but the pieces

kinda line up. Especially after Tyreke said what he said…
this is the only thing that makes any kinda twisted sense. I
mean, it's crazy as fuck, but in a way… it fits."

The group leaned in without meaning to, the hush thick
as cotton. Tyreke's impatience snapped back up like a spring.
"What makes sense?" he demanded, stepping forward. "You
gotta spell this shit out for me, man — I'm still confused."

"Just hear me out," he said, slow and steady. "The past.
That's the thread. Pull on it and everything else starts comin'
loose. After that night with Madam Linda, I went on with my
life—tried to build, tried to keep my head above water. But
somewhere along that road, Tina and me—we hit a rough
patch. Things got rocky. I ain't gonna dress it up. We both
did stupid shit. Tried to make it work, failed. And at some
point, she gave into somethin'—temptation, frustration, I
don't know which. She had… an affair. That's the ugly
truth."

He looked at Tina but kept his tone more factual than
cruel. "How I found out? I came home earlier than planned
one day. Turned down Dead Street into the cul-de-sac and
there was this smell—like smoke, hot and sharp. A car peeled
off and disappeared fast. I figured it was nothin'—not my
fight—'til I saw the house across the way was on fire. Then
I saw that white Benz in the driveway. I knew that Benz.
Tina's car. It didn't make sense—why her ride was at that
house, not mine. I pulled up out front, and some
compulsion—something in me—made me move toward it. I
couldn't explain it. Like that night in Louisiana, somethin'
pulled me in."

He swallowed. "I ran through that house. Flames hittin'
me, smoke in my lungs. I kicked open that master bedroom
door and what I found… Tina—naked—passed out from
smoke inhalation. Dre', was there too, he was fightin' for
air, fightin' to get out. Dre' and me—we'd been across the
street from each other forever. We'd talked business once,
and I turned it down. He always resented me for that. Pretty

boy, ladies' man—could always get a woman. He saw Tina, shot his shot, she was vulnerable, it happened. I scooped Tina up, put her over my shoulder, and I headed for the door."

Big D's voice got colder. "Right as I'm almost out, I hear him, screamin'. Beggin' me to come back. He's shoutin' for help. That sound…man, it cut through me. Everything in me wanted to turn. But anger was there too, burnin' under my skin. I thought about what he did to me, the disrespect, the way his choices dragged into my life. I don't know why I made the call I did. I left him. I walked out with Tina and didn't go back."

Tyreke's face went white. "Wait—wait, so… so you're sayin' you killed my uncle?" His voice trembled, trying to make the pieces move into place without the map.

Big D's eyes met his, unblinking. "I didn't kill him," he said, the words flat and awful. "But I didn't save him either. I coulda gone back. I coulda pulled him out. I didn't. I left him in that house. He died because I walked away. That's the truth."

He let that settle. "And now look at us—people I once knew gettin' picked off, my family under attack. It lines up too clean. Somebody found out what happened that night and started on a revenge tour. They're hittin' everyone close to me. Tina—remember what you told me when that fire broke out at Les's place? You said you saw a girl and a boy run out that looked like twins. You said it without knowin' all this. That ain't a coincidence. It's a pattern. Somebody connected the dots, and is takin' names, and settlin' scores—" as D was talking, a thought hit him that should have long ago.

"Wheeeeeeeeew," Crockette whistled. "Well, I'll be damned," he said, voice dripping with dry humor. "If I didn't just step right into the middle of a hot new urban drama unfolding in real time." The words hung in the air like smoke, the sting of sarcasm cutting through the heavy silence. Detective Crockette let the sarcasm hang for a beat, then straightened, the worn edge of his badge catching the moonlight. "Okay," he continued, voice sliding back into the business of it all.

"Well—we got the majority of what we need. We know where this all happened, roughly when, how, and hell, even why, in a way. We got a damn big lead on the *who,* so now it's time to act on it." He reached into his coat, thumbed a battered notepad out and tapped it with the tip of a pen. "I've heard enough backstory to night, I can go do some digging — run names, pull old incident reports, talk to people who might've known Dre'. I'll try to come up with a positive ID on the suspect, fast."

His eyes scanned each of them, steady and sharp. "But listen—we move smart. No hero shit. I haven't checked in with the precinct in hours but I'm sure by now everything is an entire shit show. We bring facts, we build a case. Y'all keep Jax quiet and out of sight until sunrise. I'll take the lead on this one."

Big D stepped closer to Crockette, his eyes sharp and serious. "Wait… I don't think you understand, Detective. We need your help—but not the kind that brings the rest of law enforcement into this. This case… It's gotta be handled off the books. Too much is at stake. And with me, Tina, and Angela still being fugitives… we can't have anyone else sniffin' around." He leaned in. "Now what we need from you is simple… get us that name. Just the name. And address if possible. Everything else—we handle ourselves. No one else can know. Got it?"

Crockette nodded.

"And… damn, with all this going on, my mind's been racin' so fast I… I let something slip. Ke'… my niece. I didn't even think about her. That's on me." He shook his head, anger and disbelief mixing in his expression. "Family's everything to me, Crockette. And I can't believe I let her situation even cross my mind this late in the game. I need you to understand—she's gotta be found, kept safe, and you're the only one who can help us with that. Since we are fugitives and Tyreke's not from around here, you're the bridge. We need that intel, and we need it clean." Big D's gaze locked on Crockette, unflinching. "This isn't about law and order no more. It's about keeping the people I care about alive. Can I count on you?"

Chapter 11

"Make A Move"

Ke' pressed her forehead against the cool window, letting the motion of the car lull her into a strange sort of numbness. Misty sat beside her, hand resting lightly over hers, while Syn leaned back with arms crossed, eyes scanning the darkened streets as if trouble could jump out from the shadows at any moment. Eric drove, quiet at first, the only sound coming from the low hum of tires over wet asphalt.

It was a quiet that felt heavy, weighted with the knowledge of everything Ke' had just learned. Her name had been broadcast on every channel, whispered through radios and televisions alike. The entire city knew of her connection to the deaths that had carved a wound straight through Hub City. She swallowed, throat tight, every breath like pulling air through a sieve. "I… I can't believe it," she murmured finally, voice barely above the car's low rumble. "They… they actually said my name. On the news."

Misty squeezed her hand, her thumb tracing slow circles over the back of Ke's hand. "It's heavy, I know. But we're here with you. You don't gotta face it alone tonight."

Ke' shook her head faintly, gaze still locked on the streaking lights outside. "But now? Now they know who I am. And they're… they're looking."

Eric's jaw tensed, eyes still on the road. "Yeah. That's the problem with running, girl. Ain't no hiding forever."

Syn added a short, sharp laugh. "Hmph, Eastside's been on edge since… since all this started. People watchin', cops watchin', and somewhere in the middle… there you are. That's the truth. You're stuck in the middle, whether you like it or not."

Ke' let out a bitter laugh, dry and shaky. "Feels more like the center of a storm."

The news report continued in the background, a low murmur of warnings and updates.

"…Authorities are torn about how to view Ke' Cook. On one hand, she is enduring unimaginable loss, as next of kin to the late Jax White… on the other, she may hold critical information regarding the sequence of attacks… residents are urged to remain indoors… authorities emphasize locating Ke' Cook is vital…"

Every word pressed down on her chest like cement. She clenched her fists in her lap, nails digging into her palms. "They don't know. I haven't done anything. They don't know anything about me or about what's really happening."

Misty's voice was soft, deliberate. "Well, you can change what they know. You can control the narrative, go with them and tell them what's what or just stay with us until we figure something else out."

Ke' turned to look at her, eyes rimmed red and wide with exhaustion. "I… I don't even know what to do anymore. Everywhere I go… it just gets worse. People keep dying, and I… I can't stop it. And I can't keep putting people in my path at risk."

Syn leaned forward slightly, her tone sharper now, tinged with impatience but not unkind. "Look, girl. You've been hiding, crying, worrying… and I get it. But I ain't gonna sugarcoat it. You gotta make a move, or they're gonna decide for you. Law enforcement and their approach as a whole, cannot be trusted, especially in a situation like this. They will try to frame you or something if they can't figure this out. That's the cold truth."

Eric cleared his throat. "Syn's right. Ain't no shame in keepin' your head down, but sooner or later, you gotta step up. Figure out a way to handle this so it don't destroy you… or the people tryin' to help you."

Misty leaned closer, voice firm now, gentle but anchored in urgency. "Ke', I gotta ask you… what do you want to do?"

Ke' pressed her hands to her face for a moment, exhaling slowly, as if the answer might burn her. Then, after a long silence, she whispered, "I… I think… I need to stop running."

All three in the front seat froze slightly, exchanging glances. Misty's eyes softened, eyebrows pulling together with concern. Are you sure, girl?"

Ke' nodded slowly, face trembling. "Yeah. I… I can't drag people into this mess. It's not fair… to anyone. I… I'll go to the precinct. Turn myself in. Just… answer their questions, do what I have to do, and… start figuring out how to survive."

"Damn. You serious?" Syn asked.

"Completely," Ke' said, voice firmer now. "I'm done hiding. Done running. I… I want to try to do it the right way. Face it head-on, instead of letting fear control me."

Eric nodded, slow and deliberate. "Alright. That's… brave. And smart. It ain't gonna be easy, but it's the right call. You'll be safe there."

Misty reached across the seat, squeezing Ke's hand one last time. "I'm proud of you for making this choice. You're not weak for turning yourself in, Ke'. You're taking control. And whatever happens in there… you ain't alone. Not completely. I'll leave you my number—just in case." She scribbled quickly on a scrap of paper from her purse, tearing it free and pressing it into Ke's hand. "Keep this. If you need anything, I mean anything…you call me. Day or night. I don't care."

Ke' looked at it, thumb brushing over the ink, eyes misting. "Thank you... really. I... I don't know how to repay you all."

Misty shook her head, smiling faintly. "A hug, maybe? And that's plenty."

Ke' let out a shaky laugh, nodding. She turned and leaned across the seat, hugging Misty, then Syn, then Eric, one by one. The embrace was brief but full of meaning, of gratitude, sorrow, and the weight of shared understanding.

"I won't forget this," Ke' whispered, voice thick with emotion. "Thank you. For everything."

Eric gave her a small nod, eyes serious but gentle. "Take care of yourself, Ke'. You hear?"

The drive to the precinct was tense and quiet, punctuated by the occasional news report echoing her name. The streets were wet, slick with rain and reflecting the orange glow of streetlights. Sirens echoed distantly, a reminder of the violence that had consumed the city.

Finally, they reached the precinct. The building loomed like a silent monolith, fluorescent lights buzzing faintly against the night sky. Ke' swallowed hard, gripping the slip of paper Misty had given her.

Misty leaned over, whispering, "You got this, Ke'. Step inside, answer the questions, and start figuring out the next move. And remember... you can call me."

Ke' nodded, giving a last half-smile to each of them. Syn's rare smile softened her usual sharp edges, and Eric offered a final, steady nod from the driver's seat.

With a deep breath, Ke' stepped out of the car, letting the door click closed behind her. She walked toward the precinct, each step a mix of fear and determination. Before she made it to the double entrance doors, she heard a voice call out her name.

***

Detective Crockette had left Big D's hideout with a weight in his chest that refused to lift. His plan was simple in theory. Return to the precinct, move as quietly as possible, and gather every shred of information they had on the possible suspect and find Ke' Cook. But simple never meant easy, not with this case. As he drove through the quiet streets, the low rumble of the engine filled the car while his mind raced through every detail, every lead, trying to assemble the puzzle into a coherent picture.

Eventually the precinct's lights came into view, flickering in the drizzle, and Crockette felt a familiar tension knot in his shoulders. Parking quickly but carefully, he exited the car and moved toward the building. His eyes were sharp, naturally scanning for any anomalies when he saw her, a young woman, moving hesitantly toward the doors. There was something immediately familiar about her posture, the way she carried herself.

He stopped for a moment, heart skipping. She was Jax White's spitting image. And then it clicked—he had seen her before, at the Cook family home, visiting after the bombing that had killed Kam. His hand went to his mouth to call out, but he hesitated, only a heartbeat.

"Ke'!" he called, his voice cutting through the damp night air.

The girl didn't respond. Either she hadn't heard him or chose to ignore it. Crockette's pace quickened, shoes splashing through puddles as he closed the distance. His voice rose, sharper this time, leaving no room for doubt. "Ke'! Wait—Ke' Cook!"

This time, she stopped. Slowly, she turned, eyes widening, fright flickering across her face. Crockette stopped a few feet away, hands raised slightly in a non-threatening gesture. "Ms. Cook! Please—wait a second! It's very important. I need to speak to you right away!" He took a cautious step closer, voice steady but urgent, carrying over the drizzle and the faint hum of the street.

Ke' froze mid-step, her hand tightening slightly on the slip of paper from Misty. She turned slowly, eyes scanning the figure in front of her, recognition dawning as she registered the badge and the determined expression. Crockette kept his hands visible, careful not to spook her, though the gravity of the night pressed in on them both.

Ke's voice was barely above a whisper. "Y-yes... sir?" she replied, eyes shifting from him to the door entrance back and forth.

Crockette's eyes softened slightly, but the urgency in his tone remained. He took another measured step closer, lowering his voice so it wouldn't carry beyond the immediate area.

"Ma'am, I know this is sudden, and I don't mean to scare you... but I need a few moments of your time. It's about your family... and what's been happening in the city."

He paused, scanning her face for any hints of fear or distrust, noting the tension in her shoulders. *She's just a kid... and yet here she is, standing right in front of me. A blessing, honestly,* he thought, *though damn, it's more than a little unnerving that she just appeared like this. Timing's so perfect. So convenient.*

His mind raced as he tried to balance caution with the necessity of speaking to her immediately. The pieces he had been trying to fit together suddenly felt a tad bit closer to connecting. "Ms. Cook... I need to ask you a few questions. It won't take long, I promise. Can we step away for a moment and have this conversation somewhere a little more private?"

Ke' hesitated, glancing at the double doors of the precinct just beyond. Her fingers twitched around the paper in her hand, but she nodded slowly, voice tentative. "Uh, o-okay... sir, but um... what's more private than one of these offices in here?" she pointed at the doors.

Crockette offered a small, reassuring nod, keeping his movements calm. Away, he knew they could talk safely—

away from the rain, away from prying eyes, and maybe, just maybe, start untangling the chaos that had engulfed her life. "Look… I know you've been through some incredibly traumatic situations, and it might be hard to trust anyone right now. But ma'am, my name is Detective Brandon Crockette. I worked closely with your brother Jax, and I'm here on his behalf—and your uncle's. Thank God I'm here at the right time, because you don't yet understand how deep this goes. I'm telling you… this is important. Before you step foot in that building, I need you to come with me."

"Excuse me… did you say my brother and my uncle?" Ke's voice trembled, disbelief and confusion rippling through her.

"Yes, ma'am," Crockette said, keeping his tone steady but urgent. "Your brother Jax… and your uncle. They're both tied up in this in ways you could never imagine. That's why I'm here—and why it's important you don't go inside right now."

Ke's eyes widened, a mix of shock and fear washing over her. "I… I don't understand… How? Why? Everything's been…"

Crockette took a careful step closer, now just inches away hands slightly raised in reassurance. "I know it's a lot, Ke'. Believe me, I get it. But coming with me is the safest way to start putting the pieces together. You're not in trouble, I'm here to help, not to hurt you. You're not alone in this and you have family waiting for you with answers you deserve."

Ke swallowed hard, hesitating for a long, tense moment, her gaze flicking toward the precinct doors, then back to him. "I… I guess… okay," she whispered finally, her voice barely audible. "I'll… I'll go with you."

***

Detective Brandon Crockette eased the cruiser into a shadowed side-street and killed the engine. The sudden silence felt louder than the rain that still beaded on the windshield. He turned in his seat and looked at Ke'—small, trembling, slip of paper clutched in her fist—like he was seeing the whole of the night through her. The streetlight washed across her face, catching the wet tracks on her cheeks. For a second, Crockette let himself simply look, the girl looked exhausted beyond her years, raw in a way that made the case stop being just a job.

Ke' sat rigid, the decision she'd made to stop running had been an act of will. Now, sitting inside a marked car, the reality of it pressed down on her.

"All right," Crockette said softly, reaching for his seat belt as if that small motion might steady both of them. "Before we get anywhere, put your seat belt on."

She fumbled with it, hands shaky. "Do I have to?"

"Yes." His voice was simple, the kind of officer tone that didn't ask. "We're not doing this half-assed. Buckle up."

She clicked the belt into place and sat back, the plastic strap a bright slash across her chest. Her fingers flexed in her lap. "Okay," she whispered. "Now what is it? You said it was important."

Crockette folded his hands on the steering wheel, breathing out slowly. "Listen to me, Ke'—and listen good. This shit is deep. Deeper than any book you've read, deeper than any movie you've seen. This ain't Hollywood. *It's real.* And the more I dig, the more I realize how long it's been underneath everybody's feet."

Her eyes blinked. "What do you mean?"

He hesitated, searching for words that wouldn't make her recoil. "I can sit here and ask you a list of questions, try to get you to tell me everything from the top, but that's not how I want to do it. And if I explain all I know—some of it you'd probably think I was making up. So, I'm not gonna do that."

Ke' swallowed, throat dry. "Then what are we gonna do?"

"There's a place I need to take you," Crockette said, eyes steady on the road even though they were still parked. "A place where your uncle is. Where people who were with your family when everything started are. We'll be with them. You'll hear things straight from folks who were there. You'll see a face or two you'll recognize. And then—maybe—it'll click. Maybe you'll begin to understand why this is happening."

Ke' let out a sound that could've been a laugh or a sob. "You think they will know what to do? I don't want to be in more trouble. I don't want to make anything worse."

"You won't be," Crockette said. "Not if you keep doing what you just did—show up and tell the truth. We're here to keep you alive." He paused for a beat and his words were slow and careful. "For now, stay calm. Trust me. The drive won't be long. Use the time to go over everything you can— names, places, dates, anything even if it feels small or stupid. When we get there, we'll talk. What you learn might change everything you thought you knew."

Ke' closed her eyes and breathed, like she was pulling breath from somewhere deep. "Okay," she said finally as the ride to her new destination proceeded.

As they were arriving, the sun was only minutes away from awaking from its nightly slumber. A faint orange hue stretched across the horizon, breaking the darkness inch by inch. The gravel and dirt cracked beneath the cruiser's tires, crunching under the slow roll as Detective Crockette steered off the main road and onto the naked back roads leading to Big D's hideaway.

Ke' sat still, her eyes fixed on the changing sky, but her body tense, shoulders locked and uneasy. Every turn the car took seemed to drag her deeper into a mystery she couldn't quite name, something in her gut told her this was no ordinary ride.

Crockette, hands tight on the wheel, kept his gaze forward, his jaw set. He didn't speak right away, letting the hum of the engine and the grinding of gravel fill the silence. But his mind was alive, thoughts rushing, running over everything that had led to this exact moment—the chaos, the revelations, the family ties tangled in blood and secrets.

Finally, he let out a breath, low and heavy. "Almost there," he muttered, more to himself than to her. Then, glancing her way, he added, "Ke', I know this road feels uncertain. I know it's hard to trust me. But what waits at the end of it… it's gonna put a lot of pieces together for you. Just hold on."

Ke' sat in her seat, chewing at her lip, her fingers drumming nervously against her thigh. "Pieces together?" she repeated quietly. "Detective, I don't even know what the whole puzzle is supposed to look like. There's no reference."

Crockette gave a dry, humorless chuckle. "Neither do I," he admitted, "But tonight… well today, we might finally get the picture."

Crockette killed the engine, the sudden silence heavy between them. He leaned back in his seat, with his eyes fixed on the farmhouse as if he was sizing up a ghost. Then, slowly, he turned toward Ke'. "I get how it looks," he said, voice low, steady. "Run-down. Empty. Like it ain't worth the risk. But trust me when I tell you—this place? It holds more answers than that precinct ever could. The uglier the cover, the deeper the truth hiding underneath. That's just how this city works." He let the words hang, watching her reaction before adding, "You said it looks worse than the situation you're in. I'm telling you… this *is* your situation. You walk inside with me, and you'll start to understand just how deep this runs."

The cruiser doors creaked open, the sound swallowed quickly by the stillness of the early morning. A faint orange glow began to smear across the horizon as the sun stretched awake. Ke' slid out cautiously, every step deliberate, her eyes sweeping over the crumbling farmhouse with uncertainty. Detective Crockette walked ahead with purpose, boots crunching over gravel as he cut around the side of the house. Ke' hesitated, arms folded tightly across her chest, then finally followed.

Rounding the back, voices drifted low in the distance. Shadows danced against the gray wood of the structure until the figures came into view. Big D stood there with others, broad frame unmistakable even in the dim light.

The moment his eyes landed on Ke', his expression broke wide with shock, then pure relief. Without a second thought, he rushed forward. "My niece!" Big D's voice cracked with emotion. In one swift move, he scooped Ke' off her feet, spinning her half around before setting her back down.

Ke' startled, heart skipping at the suddenness of it, but the warmth of his embrace cut through her unease. "Unc's so sorry, girl. I didn't mean to forget about you, leave you hangin' out there. I had no idea what all was fallin' on you. Please… forgive me." His arms tightened, rough hands trembling as he squeezed her close.

For a moment, Ke' stood frozen, then her body softened, leaning into the hug. She could feel the weight of his love pressing through the roughness of his apology, the relief radiating off him just to see her alive and standing there. Big D pulled back only enough to look her in the eyes, his own glassy with unspoken grief and gratitude. "You don't even know how happy I am to see you, girl. Alive. Well. Right here."

Before Ke' could fully process Big D's embrace, voices rose around her, filling the open space behind the farmhouse. Tina stepped forward first, eyes wide and sparkling, hands reaching out instinctively. "Ke'! Oh, my God… you're really here! Alive!" Her voice trembled with a mix of joy and disbelief, and she pulled Ke' into a careful hug, laughter and tears mingling.

Angela followed, equally elated, her arms wrapping around Ke' from the other side. "I can't believe it… you're safe! You're actually safe!" She pressed her cheek against Ke's, holding her like she would never let go.

Ke' blinked rapidly, overwhelmed by the sudden onslaught of love and relief, her chest tight with emotion. Every word, every gesture reinforced that she was no longer alone, that some part of her family had been waiting for this very moment. Then a deeper, quieter voice cut through the warm chaos. "Ke'…"

She froze, turning slowly. Tyreke was standing just a few steps away, leaning against the weathered side of the farmhouse. His presence was solid, calm, almost like a shadow grounding the scene. Her eyes widened in shock, mind racing.

"Tyreke..." she breathed, barely above a whisper. Fear and hope tangled in her chest. She had assumed the worst, imagining the fire at Jax's estate had claimed his life too. "I… I don't understand," Ke' stammered, her voice trembling as tears threatened to fall again. "I thought… I thought you were dead. The—the news… they said it was a massive fire. That they recovered at least one set of remains so far… and shell casings and—"

Tyreke stepped closer, the early morning light catching the sharp lines of his face, calm but serious. "Ke'… I made it out. Barely. But I'm here. I'm okay."

Her hands flew to her mouth, shaking, disbelief and relief warring in her chest. "But… how? How did you—"

"We'll explain everything," he said, his voice low but firm. "Right now… just know that I'm alive. And you… you're safe. That's what matters first."

Ke' swallowed hard, heart pounding. The tension in her chest eased slightly, though the questions kept crashing in. She looked at him, searching his eyes for some sign of what really happened, what they all had been through.

"I… I thought I lost everyone," she whispered.

Before Ke' could speak another word, a sharp voice cut through the tension. "It's time," Detective Crockette said, stepping forward, eyes fixed on the rising sun. "The sun is rising now… let's see if Madam Linda is right… and he is too."

Ke' froze, her gaze snapping to him. *"He… who?"* she asked, voice tight with confusion and dread.

No one answered. A tense beat passed, the morning light spilling over the group, highlighting the uneasy silence. Then Tina stepped forward, her expression shifting into quiet resolve. She reached for Ke's arm, her voice firm but calm. "He's right. Come with us."

Before she could ask anything further, Tina began leading the way, motioning for the rest of the group to follow. Slowly, deliberately, they descended into the darkness below—their footsteps echoing against the wicked, narrow steps that led down into the basement.

Ke's heart pounded as shadows swallowed them, and the air grew cooler, heavier. Every instinct screamed that the answers—and danger—waiting below would change everything.

***

The basement swallowed them in darkness almost immediately, the dim light from above fading into shadows that clung to every corner. The air was thick, carrying a musty, metallic tang that made Ke' draw a cautious breath. Her fingers gripped Tina's arm tightly, every step deliberate, careful not to trip over unseen obstacles.

A faint noise echoed somewhere deeper in the basement, and Ke' froze. The sound didn't come from any of the people around her. It was something else. Something deliberate. Her pulse quickened. "Stay close," Tina whispered, voice low but commanding.

Ke' nodded, swallowing hard. She could hear the others' footsteps behind her, muted but steady. Each step seemed to carry them further into uncertainty, the walls closing in as if the basement itself were alive, waiting to see what they would do next.

A low light appeared ahead, weak but enough to reveal shapes—furniture stacked haphazardly, old crates, a workbench cluttered with tools and papers. Something about the place felt rehearsed, almost like it had been waiting for them.

Big D's voice broke the silence, low and cautious. "Everyone… quiet. Let her see this first."

Ke' glanced up at him, eyes wide. "See what?" He gave her shoulder a reassuring squeeze.

"You'll see. Just keep walking." She followed slowly, every step deliberate as the basement swallowed them in darkness. "Almost there… just a few more steps."

The group moved in a tight circle, forming a loose line as they navigated the basement.

Ke's eyes flicked to the shapes around her, stacked crates, a rusted workbench, tools scattered like the remnants of forgotten lives. And then she noticed it—an old table at the center of the basement. Something under a white sheet lay draped across it.

Ke's breath caught. "W-what… what is that?" she whispered, voice trembling.

Tina's hand went up, pressing gently against Ke's arm. "Shhh… watch."

The group fell silent, forming a protective semi-circle around the table. Even in the dim light, the contours of a body beneath the sheet were unmistakable, but nothing moved at first.

Ke' felt her pulse hammer in her ears as she took a tentative step closer, her eyes widening with a mixture of fear and curiosity.

Upon closer inspection, the sheet began to move slightly, rising and falling as if something beneath it was breathing. Ke's fingers clutched Tina's arm tighter. "Is… is it… alive?"

Tina gave a small shake of her head but said nothing. The rest of the group remained still, faces tense yet unreadable. Every second felt like it stretched into eternity.

Then suddenly, the body under the sheet snapped upright, the fabric falling away in a cascade of white, revealing… someone Ke' didn't expect. Her mouth fell open, heart stopping. She stumbled backward, eyes wide as the figure stood fully before her.

The room was still for a heartbeat, everyone holding their breath, They had known this moment was coming.

Ke' could only scream, a sharp, raw sound of disbelief and shock tearing from her throat. "Oh my God!"

TO BE CONTINUED…

**FOR A SNEAK PEEK OF
HUB CITY MENACE 5: DEATH PREVAILS
CONTINUE READING**

Chapter 1

"The Son Is Risen"

Ke's breath hitched in her throat. Her legs nearly gave out, and her hands trembled as she stumbled forward through the half-light of the basement. "Oh... my... God!" she gasped, voice breaking under the weight of disbelief, fear, and something like deliverance.

The room held its breath as she dropped to her knees beside him. Jax lay still—chest bare under the dim light, wrapped in a sheet that clung to his frame like burial cloth. His skin was cold, but not lifeless. There was a hum to him, something just beneath the surface, like the world itself was waiting for him to breathe.

Ke pressed a shaking hand to his face. "Jax..." Her voice cracked. The sound barely escaped her lips. "Jax, please—please open your eyes, brother."

Her tears fell hot against his skin. The others watched in a silence that felt ancient. Big D stood stiff, his broad frame a mount for everyone else. Tina clutched Angela's hand harder without realizing it. Tyreke stared like he was seeing a ghost. Even Detective Crockette, ever the skeptic but yet hopeful, couldn't mask the fear crawling up his spine.

And then—as Ke' reached and touched her unmoving brother, there was a sound. A gasp that cut through the quiet like thunder through the night. Jax's chest rose with a sharp inhale, air ripping back into his lungs like the world owed him breath. His body jerked once, twice—then stilled. The sheet slid from the rest of his body, exposing himself bare to all just like the first day he was born. His fingers and arms twitched. Then his eyes snapped open.

It wasn't shock.

It was *awareness.*

His gaze burned alive, wild and focused all at once, like someone who'd just seen everything that ever mattered—and everything that ever hurt. The pupils constricted, then widened, and in that split second, every memory, every betrayal, every scream, every bullet, every flame—crashed back into him. The moment between realms was gone. He was here now. And he remembered *everything.*

Ke cried out and threw her arms around him. "You're alive—oh my God, you're really—" she began to pick herself up and reach for him until her words broke off as she felt his body trembling—not from weakness, but from a clear internal fury that radiated off him now like heat. His breath was heavy, deep, almost animal.

Jax's voice came out low and rough, cutting through her sobs. "Ke…" He swallowed hard, his jaw tightening. "Get back a little." The tone in his voice made her freeze. It wasn't unkind—but it was commanding, certain. It was the voice of someone who'd just returned from a place no one comes back from.

He pushed himself up slowly, every muscle flexing as if his body were reintroducing itself to gravity. His bare feet planted firm against the cold concrete. It appeared as if steam rose faintly from his skin, like the air itself recoiled from the energy pulsing through him.

Big D took a cautious step forward. "*Nephew…?*"

Jax's head lifted. His eyes found him, sharp and full of something ancient. "*I know,*" he said definitively.

No one moved.

Jax scanned the room—Ke, Big D, Tyreke, Tina, Angela, Crockette. His chest heaved, not from fear but from the rawness of being alive again. "I know who shot me. I know why. I know every reason this shit started." He clenched his fists until his knuckles cracked. "*Everything… is my fault.*"

The room's air thickened, charged with the kind of silence that only comes before a storm.

Ke shook her head slowly, tears streaming. "Brother, please...Don't—"

He gave her a signal to pause, looked at her then, really looked, and the rage softened—just for a heartbeat. But guilt flashed behind his eyes. "You shouldn't've have been a part of this." His voice cracked, heavy with shame. "I know it all, Ke. Before I was shot... Before that muthafucka tried to kill me, he told me *everything.*"

Big D started to speak, but Jax's stare cut him off.

"I've already seen it from the other side, and it's ugly." The words hung heavy. Everyone felt them, even if they didn't fully understand what he meant. "You ever been somewhere between a heartbeat and forever? Where everything makes sense—every lie, every death, every reason you still breathe?" He let out a breath, slow and bitter. "That's where I was. And I saw what's comin'."

Silence.

Then Jax straightened fully, squaring his shoulders. The fear in the room was replaced by something else. Anticipation.

He looked around one last time, meeting each of their eyes. "A long time ago, I did something I had no clue would cause this much damage." The lights flickered. Somewhere above them, thunder rolled across the city. "Unintentionally, my past actions sparked a personal war from a very vengeful individual who created the reality we are all facing today."

Ke stared, breathless. "Jax... what are you gonna do?"

With zero hesitation and all seriousness Jax's eyes hardened, but his voice was calm, almost too calm. *"Finish it."*

Hub City Menace 4: Immortal Gangstas
QUESTIONNAIRE

Chapter 1:
1. What two visitors arrive at Jax's mansion shortly after he finishes his phone call with Terry, and what is the significance of each in this chapter? (Checks attention to character introductions and their context in the plot.)
2. During the confrontation with Terry, what object does he reveal to Jax that triggers the flood of memories, and what is the number displayed on it? (Ensures readers caught the key symbolic moment and the supernatural/psychological tension introduced.)

Chapter 2:
1. What specific actions does Terry claim to have orchestrated against Jax's loved ones, and how does he reveal them during the confrontation? (Tests attention to the details of Terry's confession and the stakes for Jax's family.)
2. What object does Terry use to trap Jax at the end of the chapter, and what does this action symbolize in the context of their conflict? (Ensures readers caught the climactic tension and the symbolic meaning behind Terry's actions.)

Chapter 3:
1. What realization does Tyreke come to about the intruder during the fire, and how does this change his understanding of the situation? (Checks that readers noticed the family connection twist and the emotional weight it carries.)
2. How does Terry—or the intruder—use the environment and objects in the mansion to try to

control or harm Jax, and what nearly happens as a result? (Ensures readers followed the scene with the accelerant, fire, and the life-threatening danger to Jax.)

Chapter 4:

1. How does Detective Crockette's prior relationship with Jax influence his decisions when encountering Big D and the injured Jax?(Checks comprehension of character backstory and how it drives current action.)
2. Compare the reactions of Angela and Tina to Big D's actions. What do their responses reveal about their beliefs and past experiences? (Encourages analysis of perspective and emotional response to the supernatural events.)

Chapter 5:

1. How does the news report about the fire trigger Ke's suspicion, and what specific details lead her to connect Terry to the crime? (Ensures readers recognized the arson clues, spent shell casing, and Terry's suspicious behavior.)
2. In what ways does Terry manipulate Ke' emotionally during the scene, and how does this false sense of comfort heighten the tension of the chapter? (Verifies that readers understood his calculated deception and the psychological control he exerts.)

Chapter 6:

1. How does the city react to the news of Jax's likely death, and what does this reveal about his influence and significance within the community? (Checks that readers understood the social and emotional impact of Jax's role.)

2. How does Ke' navigate the chaos during the riots, and what is the significance of Misty, Eric, and Syn in her moment of vulnerability? (Ensures readers noticed her fear, physical strain, and the human kindness that aids her survival.)

Chapter 7:
1. How does Tory confront Terry about his actions, and what specific mistakes of his did she highlight that put them both at risk? (Checks that readers understood the tension between the siblings and Terry's reckless behavior.)

2. What does Tory's reaction reveal about her priorities and her role in the plan, especially regarding the potential survivors and Ke'? (Ensures readers recognized her strategic thinking and protective instincts.)

Chapter 8:
1. What extreme measures do Tina and the group take to try to save Jax, and how does Madam Linda's intervention change the dynamic of the scene? (Checks that readers understood the ritual, Tina's reluctant participation, and the supernatural element introduced.)
2. How do the reactions of Tyreke, Angela, and Crockette emphasize the tension and stakes of Jax's condition during the ritual? (Ensures readers noticed the emotional weight and suspense surrounding his near-death state.)

Chapter 9:
1. How does the group of strangers—Misty, Eric, and Syn—react to Ke's distress, and what does their behavior reveal about their characters? (Checks that

readers noticed the dynamics of trust, empathy, and caution in this tense rescue scene.)

2. What is the significance of Ke' Cook being publicly identified as Jax White's next of kin, and how does this revelation escalate the tension in the story? (Ensures readers understood the stakes for Ke' and the city, as well as the implications of her newfound prominence.)

Chapter 10:
1. How does Big D's revelation about Madam Linda's ritual and the resulting "physical immortality" affect the group's perception of the danger they are facing, and how does it influence their sense of urgency? (Encourages readers to reflect on how supernatural elements heighten stakes and character responsibility.)
2. How does the revelation about Tina's past, the affair, and the fire contribute to the larger narrative of revenge and justice, and how does it complicate the characters' relationships? (Ensures readers grasp the intertwined personal and familial conflicts driving the story forward.)

Chapter 11:
1. Ke' decides to stop running and face the authorities after a long internal struggle. What do you think motivates her to finally make this choice, and how do Misty, Syn, and Eric influence her decision?
2. When Ke' arrives at Big D's hideout and sees her family and Tyreke alive, how does this moment affect her emotionally, and what does it reveal about the importance of family and trust in this chapter?

Lock Down Publications and Ca$h Presents
Assisted Publishing Packages

Due to an increase in the price of services we have increased our prices. The prices below reflect the price increase as of 11/1/24.

BASIC PACKAGE	UPGRADED PACKAGE
$699	**$1000**
Editing	Typing
Cover Design	Editing
Formatting	Cover Design
	Formatting
	Upload eBooks to Amazon
	Upload Paperback to Amazon
ADVANCE PACKAGE	**LDP SUPREME PACKAGE**
$1,400	**$1,700**
Typing	Typing
Editing (line editing/content)	Editing (line editing/content)
Cover Design	Cover Design
Formatting	Formatting
Copyright Registration	Copyright Registration
Proofreading	Proofreading
Upload eBooks to Amazon	Set up Amazon Account
Upload Paperback to Amazon	Upload eBooks to Amazon
	Upload Paperback to Amazon
	Advertise on LDP's Amazon and Facebook Page

***

Other services available upon request.
Additional charges may apply

Lock Down Publications
P.O. Box 944
Stockbridge, GA 30281-9998
Phone: 470 303-9761
Email: lockdownpublications@gmail.com

Submission Guideline

Submit the first three chapters of your completed manuscript to ldpsubmissions@gmail.com. In the subject line add **Your Book's Title**. The manuscript must be in a Word Doc file and sent as an attachment. Document should be in Times New Roman, double spaced, and in size 12 font. Also, provide your synopsis and full contact information. If sending multiple submissions, they must each be in a separate email.

Have a story but no way to send it electronically? You can still submit to LDP/Ca$h Presents. Send in the first three chapters, written or typed, of your completed manuscript to:

LDP: Submissions Dept
P.O. Box 944
Stockbridge, GA 30281-9998

DO NOT send original manuscript. Must be a duplicate.
Provide your synopsis and a cover letter containing your full contact information.

Thanks for considering LDP and Ca$h Presents.

NEW RELEASES

BLOODLINE OF A SAVAGE 1-3
THESE VICIOUS STREETS 1-3
RELENTLESS GOON 1-3
BY PRINCE A. TAUHID

THE BUTTERFLY MAFIA 1-3
BY FUMIYA PAYNE

A THUG'S STREET PRINCESS 1&2
BY MEESHA

CITY OF SMOKE 3
BY MOLOTTI

GET IT IN SLUGS 1 &2
BY B. STALL

STANDING ON HER BUSINESS 1&2
BY DG SANTANA

STEPPERS 1,2&3
THE REAL BADDIES OF CHI-RAQ
BY KING RIO

THE LANE 1&2
BY KEN-KEN SPENCE

THUG OF SPADES 1&2
LOVE IN THE TRENCHES 2
CORNER BOYS
BY COREY ROBINSON

TIL DEATH 3
BY ARYANNA

HUB CITY MENACE 4 | J. WHITE

THE BIRTH OF A GANGSTER 4
BY DELMONT PLAYER

PRODUCT OF THE STREETS 1-3
BY DEMOND "MONEY" ANDERSON

NO TIME FOR ERROR
BY KEESE

MONEY HUNGRY DEMONS 1-2
BY TRANAY ADAMS

HUB CITY MENACE 1-3
BY J. WHITE

A THUGGISH PASSION 1&2
LAND OF DA HOOLIGANZ 1-4
KILLAZ ON STANDBY 1&2
BY IRA B.

FO'EVA ROLLIN 1&2
BY ASSA RAYMOND BAKER

THE LEVEL UP 1&3
BY LUXURY KING

Coming Soon from Lock Down Publications/Ca$h Presents

IF YOU CROSS ME ONCE 6
ANGEL V
By Anthony Fields

A THUGS STREET PRINCESS 3
By Meesha

CORNER BOYS 2
By Corey Robinson

THA TAKEOVER
By Keith Chandler

BETRAYAL OF A G 2
By Ray Vinci

SAVAGE FAMILY EMPIRE 1&2
SOULLESS GOON 1,2&3
THE DIRTY SIDE OF MONEY 1,2&3
By Prince

FOR MY ENEMY'S SAKE
AMBITIONS OF A SLIDER
FRESH OFF DA PORCH
By IRA B.

BY THE TRUCKLOAD 1-4
TIPPIN' THE SCALES 1-3
BAD BITCHES WIT GUNZ 3
PROBLEM SOLVED 2
By Christopher "Diesel" Hornezes

Available Now

RESTRAINING ORDER 1 & 2
By **CA$H & Coffee**

LOVE KNOWS NO BOUNDARIES 1-3
By **Coffee**

RAISED AS A GOON I, II, III & IV
BRED BY THE SLUMS I, II, III
BLAST FOR ME I & II
ROTTEN TO THE CORE I II III
A BRONX TALE I, II, III
DUFFLE BAG CARTEL I II III IV V VI
HEARTLESS GOON I II III IV V
A SAVAGE DOPEBOY I II
DRUG LORDS I II III
CUTTHROAT MAFIA I II
KING OF THE TRENCHES
By **Ghost**

LAY IT DOWN I & II
LAST OF A DYING BREED I II
BLOOD STAINS OF A SHOTTA I & II III
By **Jamaica**

LOYAL TO THE GAME I II III
LIFE OF SIN I, II III
By **TJ & Jelissa**

IF LOVING HIM IS WRONG…I & II
LOVE ME EVEN WHEN IT HURTS I II III
By **Jelissa**

PUSH IT TO THE LIMIT
By **Bre' Hayes**

BLOODY COMMAS I & II
SKI MASK CARTEL I, II & III
KING OF NEW YORK I II, III IV V
RISE TO POWER I II III
COKE KINGS I II III IV V
BORN HEARTLESS I II III IV
KING OF THE TRAP I II
By **T.J. Edwards**

WHEN THE STREETS CLAP BACK I & II III
THE HEART OF A SAVAGE I II III IV
MONEY MAFIA I II
LOYAL TO THE SOIL I II III
By **Jibril Williams**

A DISTINGUISHED THUG STOLE MY HEART I II & III
LOVE SHOULDN'T HURT I II III IV
RENEGADE BOYS 1-4
PAID IN KARMA 1-3
SAVAGE STORMS 1-3
AN UNFORESEEN LOVE 1-3
BABY, I'M WINTERTIME COLD 1-3
A THUG'S STREET PRINCESS 1&2
By **Meesha**

A GANGSTER'S CODE 1-3
A GANGSTER'S SYN 1-3
THE SAVAGE LIFE 1-3
CHAINED TO THE STREETS 1-3
BLOOD ON THE MONEY 1-3
A GANGSTA'S PAIN 1-3
BEAUTIFUL LIES AND UGLY TRUTHS
CHURCH IN THESE STREETS
By **J-Blunt**

CUM FOR ME 1-8
An LDP Erotica Collaboration

HUB CITY MENACE 4 | J. WHITE

BLOOD OF A BOSS 1-5
SHADOWS OF THE GAME
TRAP BASTARD
By **Askari**

THE STREETS BLEED MURDER 1-3
THE HEART OF A GANGSTA 1-3
By **Jerry Jackson**

WHEN A GOOD GIRL GOES BAD
By **Adrienne**

THE COST OF LOYALTY 1-3
By **Kweli**

BRIDE OF A HUSTLA 1-3
THE FETTI GIRLS 1-3
CORRUPTED BY A GANGSTA 1-4
BLINDED BY HIS LOVE
THE PRICE YOU PAY FOR LOVE 1-3
DOPE GIRL MAGIC 1-3
By **Destiny Skai**

A KINGPIN'S AMBITION
A KINGPIN'S AMBITION II
I MURDER FOR THE DOUGH
By **Ambitious**

TRUE SAVAGE 1-7
DOPE BOY MAGIC 1-3
MIDNIGHT CARTEL 1-3
CITY OF KINGZ 1&2
NIGHTMARE ON SILENT AVE
THE PLUG OF LIL MEXICO 1&2
CLASSIC CITY
By **Chris Green**

A GANGSTER'S REVENGE 1-4
THE BOSS MAN'S DAUGHTERS 1-5
A SAVAGE LOVE 1&2
BAE BELONGS TO ME 1&2
A HUSTLER'S DECEIT 1-3
WHAT BAD BITCHES DO 1-3
SOUL OF A MONSTER 1-3
KILL ZONE
A DOPE BOY'S QUEEN 1-3
TIL DEATH 1-3
IMMA DIE BOUT MINE 1-6
DYING FOR LIKES
By **Aryanna**

A DOPEBOY'S PRAYER
By **Eddie "Wolf" Lee**

THE KING CARTEL 1-3
By **Frank Gresham**

THESE NIGGAS AIN'T LOYAL 1-3
By **Nikki Tee**

GANGSTA SHYT 1-3
By **CATO**

THE ULTIMATE BETRAYAL
By **Phoenix**

BOSS'N UP 1-3
By **Royal Nicole**

I LOVE YOU TO DEATH
By **Destiny J**

I RIDE FOR MY HITTA
I STILL RIDE FOR MY HITTA
By **Misty Holt**

LOVE & CHASIN' PAPER
By **Qay Crockett**

TO DIE IN VAIN
SINS OF A HUSTLA
By **ASAD**

BROOKLYN HUSTLAZ
By **Boogsy Morina**

BROOKLYN ON LOCK 1 & 2
By **Sonovia**

GANGSTA CITY
By **Teddy Duke**

A DRUG KING AND HIS DIAMOND 1-3
A DOPEMAN'S RICHES
HER MAN, MINE'S TOO 1&2
CASH MONEY HO'S
THE WIFEY I USED TO BE 1&2
PRETTY GIRLS DO NASTY THINGS
By **Nicole Goosby**

LIPSTICK KILLAH 1-3
CRIME OF PASSION 1-3
FRIEND OR FOE 1-3
By **Mimi**

TRAPHOUSE KING 1-3
KINGPIN KILLAZ 1-3
STREET KINGS 1&2
PAID IN BLOOD 1&2
CARTEL KILLAZ 1-3
DOPE GODS 1&2
By **Hood Rich**

THE STREETS ARE CALLING
By **Duquie Wilson**

STEADY MOBBN' 1-3
THE STREETS STAINED MY SOUL 1-3
By **Marcellus Allen**

WHO SHOT YA 1-3
SON OF A DOPE FIEND 1-4
HEAVEN GOT A GHETTO 1&2
SKI MASK MONEY 1&2
By **Renta**

GORILLAZ IN THE BAY 1-4
TEARS OF A GANGSTA 1/&2
3X KRAZY 1&2
STRAIGHT BEAST MODE 1&2
By **DE'KARI**

TRIGGADALE 1-3
MURDA WAS THE CASE 1-3
By **Elijah R. Freeman**

SLAUGHTER GANG 1-3
RUTHLESS HEART 1-3
By **Willie Slaughter**

GOD BLESS THE TRAPPERS 1-3
THESE SCANDALOUS STREETS 1-3
FEAR MY GANGSTA 1-5
THESE STREETS DON'T LOVE NOBODY 1-2
BURY ME A G 1-5
A GANGSTA'S EMPIRE 1-4
THE DOPEMAN'S BODYGAURD 1&2
THE REALEST KILLAZ 1-3
THE LAST OF THE OGS 1-3
By **Tranay Adams**

MARRIED TO A BOSS 1-3
By **Destiny Skai & Chris Green**

KINGZ OF THE GAME 1-7
CRIME BOSS 1-4
By **Playa Ray**

FUK SHYT
By **Blakk Diamond**

DON'T F#CK WITH MY HEART 1&2
By **Linnea**

ADDICTED TO THE DRAMA 1-3
IN THE ARM OF HIS BOSS
By **Jamila**

LOYALTY AIN'T PROMISED 1&2
By **Keith Williams**

YAYO 1-4
A SHOOTER'S AMBITION 1&2
BRED IN THE GAME
By **S. Allen**

TRAP GOD 1-3
RICH $AVAGE 1-3
MONEY IN THE GRAVE 1-3
CARTEL MONEY 1&2
By **Martell Troublesome Bolden**

FOREVER GANGSTA 1&2
GLOCKS ON SATIN SHEETS 1&2
By **Adrian Dulan**

TOE TAGZ 1-4
LEVELS TO THIS SHYT 1&2
IT'S JUST ME AND YOU
By **Ah'Million**

KINGPIN DREAMS 1-3
RAN OFF ON DA PLUG
By **Paper Boi Rari**

THE STREETS MADE ME 1-3
By **Larry D. Wright**

CONFESSIONS OF A GANGSTA 1-4
CONFESSIONS OF A JACKBOY 1-3
CONFESSIONS OF A HITMAN
CONFESSIONS OF A DOPE BOY
By **Nicholas Lock**

I'M NOTHING WITHOUT HIS LOVE
SINS OF A THUG
TO THE THUG I LOVED BEFORE
A GANGSTA SAVED XMAS
IN A HUSTLER I TRUST
By **Monet Dragun**

QUIET MONEY 1-3
THUG LIFE 1-3
EXTENDED CLIP 1&2
A GANGSTA'S PARADISE
By **Trai'Quan**

CAUGHT UP IN THE LIFE 1-3
THE STREETS NEVER LET GO 1-3
By **Robert Baptiste**

NEW TO THE GAME 1-3
MONEY, MURDER & MEMORIES 1-3
By **Malik D. Rice**

CREAM 2-3
THE STREETS WILL TALK
By **Yolanda Moore**

THE STREETS WILL NEVER CLOSE 1-3
By **K'ajji**

LIFE OF A SAVAGE 1-4
A GANGSTA'S QUR'AN 1-4
MURDA SEASON 1-3
GANGLAND CARTEL 1-3
CHI'RAQ GANGSTAS 1-4
KILLERS ON ELM STREET 1-3
JACK BOYZ N DA BRONX 1-3
A DOPEBOY'S DREAM 1-3
JACK BOYS VS DOPE BOYS 1-3
COKE GIRLZ
COKE BOYS
SOSA GANG 1&2
BRONX SAVAGES
BODYMORE KINGPINS
BLOOD OF A GOON
By **Romell Tukes**

CONCRETE KILLA 1-3
VICIOUS LOYALTY 1-3
BLOODY MONEY BAGS
By **Kingpen**

THE ULTIMATE SACRIFICE 1-6
KHADIFI
IF YOU CROSS ME ONCE 1-3
ANGEL 1-4
IN THE BLINK OF AN EYE
By **Anthony Fields**

THE LIFE OF A HOOD STAR
By **Ca$h & Rashia Wilson**

NIGHTMARES OF A HUSTLA 1-3
BLOOD AND GAMES 1&2
By **King Dream**

GHOST MOB
By **Stilloan Robinson**

HARD AND RUTHLESS 1&2
MOB TOWN 251
THE BILLIONAIRE BENTLEYS 1-3
REAL G'S MOVE IN SILENCE
By **Von Diesel**

MOB TIES 1-7
SOUL OF A HUSTLER, HEART OF A KILLER 1-3
GORILLAZ IN THE TRENCHES
OOPS CRY TOO 1&2
THE DAUGHTER OF A CARTEL BOSS
By **SayNoMore**

BODYMORE MURDERLAND 1-3
THE BIRTH OF A GANGSTER 1-4
By **Delmont Player**

FOR THE LOVE OF A BOSS 1&2
By **C. D. Blue**

KILLA KOUNTY 1-5
TENDER
By **Khufu**

MOBBED UP 1-4
THE BRICK MAN 1-5
THE COCAINE PRINCESS 1-10
STEPPERS 1-3
SUPER GREMLIN 1-4
A GANGSTA'S SON
By **King Rio**

MONEY GAME 1&2
By **Smoove Dolla**

A GANGSTA'S KARMA 1-5
By **FLAME**

KING OF THE TRENCHES 1-3
By **GHOST & TRANAY ADAMS**

BAD BITCHES WIT GUNZ 1&2
PROBLEM SOLVED
By "Christopher Diesel" Hornezes

QUEEN OF THE ZOO 1&2
By **Black Migo**

GRIMEY WAYS 1-3
BETRAYAL OF A G
By **Ray Vinci**

XMAS WITH AN ATL SHOOTER
By **Ca$h & Destiny Skai**

KING KILLA 1&2
By **Vincent "Vitto" Holloway**

BETRAYAL OF A THUG 1&2
By **Fre$h**

COUNTDOWN OF A KILLA 1&2
SEX, MURDER AND GOD 1&2
GUNS DOWN, BOTTOMS UP 1&2
By Lo-Life

THE MURDER QUEENS 1-7
By **Michael Gallon**

FOR THE LOVE OF BLOOD 1-4
By **Jamel Mitchell**

HUB CITY MENACE 4 | J. WHITE

HUB CITY MENACE 4 | J. WHITE

THE BUTTERFLY MAFIA 1-3
SALUTE MY SAVAGERY 1&2
By **Fumiya Payne**

THE LANE 1&2
By Ken-Ken Spence

THE PUSSY TRAP 1-5
By **Nene Capri**

DIRTY DNA
By **Blaque**

SANCTIFIED AND HORNY
by **XTASY**

BOOKS BY LDP'S CEO, CA$H

TRUST IN NO MAN
TRUST IN NO MAN 2
TRUST IN NO MAN 3
BONDED BY BLOOD
SHORTY GOT A THUG
THUGS CRY
THUGS CRY 2
THUGS CRY 3
TRUST NO BITCH
TRUST NO BITCH 2
TRUST NO BITCH 3
TIL MY CASKET DROPS
RESTRAINING ORDER
RESTRAINING ORDER 2
IN LOVE WITH A CONVICT
LIFE OF A HOOD STAR
XMAS WITH AN ATL SHOOTER

www.ingramcontent.com/pod-product-compliance
Lightning Source LLC
Chambersburg PA
CBHW060427260626
47161CB00005B/1810